Mary Bennet and the Bloomsbury Coven

Beth Deitchman

Copyright © 2014 Beth Deitchman

All rights reserved.

Luminous Creatures Press

Cover design by Streetlight Graphics

ISBN-13: 978-1502905185

Luminous Creatures Press Books:

The Velocipede Races
By Emily June Street

Secret Room
by Emily June Street

The Painted Dog and Other Stories
By Beth Deitchman & Emily June Street

Ungodly Hungers
By Beth Deitchman & Emily June Street

Margaret Dashwood and the Enchanted Atlas
By Beth Deitchman

Coming Soon:

The Gantean
By Emily June Street

CHAPTER I

*M*ary Bennet's spectacles slid down her nose as she lowered her face toward her book. With an impatient gesture, she pushed them back into place and resumed reading. Her attention had been diverted by her father's entrance into the drawing room. As a rule, Mr. Bennet preferred to retire after dinner to the solitude of his library, avoiding what he considered the "noisy chatter" of Longbourn's women. This evening, however, he had surprised his family by joining them. Ignoring their curious stares, he had taken a chair near the fire and disappeared behind his newspaper, displaying little interest in the activities of his wife and daughters. By the time her father had opened his paper, Mary had already forgotten the interruption, so lost was she in her book's excitement. Although she had retraced the steps of Emily St. Aubert many times before, the poor heroine's fate never failed to make Mary's heart pound.

Had her family known that the book now spread on her lap was not Fordyce's Sermons but Mrs.

Radcliffe's *The Mysteries of Udolpho*, Mary would have faced no end of teasing. Her opinion of novels, having been repeatedly and forcefully stated, was well known to the entire Bennet family, none of whom would have thought to present her with such a book. Instead it had been a gift from the dashing Captain Wickham, husband to Mary's youngest sister Lydia, who knew nothing about her opinions. Mary's response to his gift had been less than gracious: "I must say, my dear sir, I had thought better of you. There is no value or self-improvement to be gained, no lesson to be learned from wasting one's time buried in a fiction. No, no, reading to improve one's mind requires material of far more weight and depth."

Not prone to concerning himself with self-improvement, Wickham had laughed and patted Mary on the shoulder, saying with good humor, "Dearest sister, I think you should allow Mrs. Radcliffe the opportunity to convince you otherwise. There are just as many lessons to be learned from a novel as from a sermon, especially for a young woman such as you."

Mary had not understood his meaning, but her native curiosity, so long suppressed by notions of what she *should* be rather than what she *could* be, had been piqued. "Mr. Wickham has taken great pains to bring me this book. It would be rude of me not to examine it," she said one afternoon when she was alone in the drawing room with nothing to read. "At the very least it will provide matter for an extract on the dangers of novel reading," she concluded, satisfied with her reasoning.

Her disdain soon gave way to delight as she found herself, almost against her will, completely absorbed by the story. And while in principle she had disapproved of her brother-in-law's gesture as perhaps over-stepping the bounds of good taste, once exposed to the thrill of the novel, her opinion of him had softened considerably.

On the rare occasions when their paths crossed, Mr. Wickham had enquired about Mary's progress through the book. His kind attention, which Mary had misinterpreted as a sign of deeper interest, led Mary into feelings she had never before entertained. To her despair, she came to believe herself in love with a man who must always remain out of her reach—his heart having been eternally pledged to her sister Lydia—and for the first time in her life, Mary had known the sharp pangs of heartbreak. She had taken solace in repeated readings of *The Mysteries of Udolpho*, cherishing the bittersweet sentiments the book aroused in her. Soon enough the dry sermons and religious poetry that she had long favored were forever displaced by novels.

The third girl of five, Mary had no great beauty or native wit to recommend her, as had her older sisters Jane and Elizabeth. Nor had she a carefree or excitable nature, like that of her younger sisters Lydia and Catherine. Mary was plain and sometimes awkward. But rather than submit to a life without distinction, she had made a concerted effort to develop her musical skills and her intellect. Regrettably, she undertook these tasks without guidance from a parent or a teacher and developed several unfortunate habits. While she played the *pianoforte* with some technical skill, her music was bereft of real feeling, and she read without true understanding, which should have prevented her from discoursing at length about her books. Her family learned to ignore her pretentions.

But when she started reading novels, Mary experienced an exhilaration completely new to her—her long dormant imagination, which no one had taken the trouble to foster, had awakened. Perhaps Mr. Wickham had seen some hint of fancy in Mary's eyes that had inspired his gift. More likely he simply wished to seek favor with every member of the family and thought by presenting Mary with a book, he might secure her good opinion. Nevertheless, whatever his motives, he had, in more ways than one, transformed Mary's life.

On this particular evening, Mary once again occupied herself with Captain Wickham's gift. So absorbed was she by poor Miss St. Aubert's adventures that she failed to hear her mother calling her name until Mrs. Bennet was standing right in front her.

"Mary. For heaven's sake, I have been calling you *endlessly*," complained Mrs. Bennet.

"Mrs. Bennet, let us not exaggerate. You have called Mary exactly three times, twice from the hall, so the poor child could barely hear you," said her husband from behind his newspaper.

"Well, however many times I have called, I have your attention now. This package has come for you in the evening post." Mrs. Bennet thrust a rectangular object wrapped in plain brown paper toward her daughter. Mary took it and set it on the table next to her, leaving it wrapped. She had no desire to reveal its contents to anyone in her family.

"Go ahead and open it," cried Mrs. Bennet, impatient to see what was inside.

Knowing her mother would not soon be distracted

from her curiosity, Mary relented and unwrapped the package, revealing a small quarto with a worn red cover.

"Oh, it is just another book," said Mrs. Bennet. "I do not know why I should have been so excited." She took her seat opposite her husband and picked up her needlework. "Well? Are we to know what great work you shall read next?"

"Another collection of John Donne's sermons," replied Mary. "Shall I read one aloud?"

"That will not be necessary, my dear," Mr. Bennet hastened to answer. "I find such matter is best enjoyed in solitude."

Smiling to herself, Mary returned to her book, pleased by the easy deflection of her parents' attention. She knew from long experience that no one cared to hear her read aloud. It was just as well, for the book in question, *A Sicilian Romance* by Mrs. Radcliffe, contained not a single sermon. She had awaited its arrival from a bookshop in London with great anticipation and forced herself to resist its tempting presence on the table next to her. So as Mrs. Bennet and Kitty chattered about the next morning's shopping in Meryton and her father rustled though his paper, Mary tried to bend her mind toward *The Mysteries of Udolpho*, absorbing very little of what she read.

When the bells in the little mantel clock chimed across the drawing room, Mary looked up.

"Goodness, it has grown late," exclaimed Mrs. Bennet. "Mary, Kitty, it is time for you to go to bed. And Mary, please do not sit up reading until all hours of the night. You will get a terrible squint."

Mary rose, happy for the excuse to retire to her

room where she could read her new book in private. She bid her parents good night and left the drawing room. Before Jane and Elizabeth had the fortune to marry so well, Mary had occupied a small room adjacent to the one shared by her younger sisters, Kitty and Lydia. She found pleasure in pretending that tiny room was a poet's garret where she passed many happy hours reading and writing in relative peace. However, after Jane's marriage to Mr. Bingley and Elizabeth's to Mr. Darcy, Mary was granted permission to move into the bigger room once shared by the eldest Bennet girls. From time to time she felt her sisters' absence, especially Elizabeth's, but she had grown fond of her new room; not only did it provide ample space for her belongings and a better view of Longbourn's woodlands, but it also afforded her long-desired privacy, removing her as it did from Kitty's vicinity. In this room she often sat looking out the window and dreaming of a life far away from the tedium of Hertfordshire.

Upon reaching her room Mary went about her nightly ablutions, got into bed, and blew out her candle. In the dark she listened with mounting impatience for signs that the rest of her family had retired. At last, after an agonizing wait, she heard the final door close. She sighed, realizing that she had been holding her breath. Then she got out of bed and arranged a blanket against the bottom of her door to prevent any light from leaking into the hallway and betraying her purpose. When she felt herself safe from discovery, she re-lit her candle and, propped comfortably in her bed, opened her new book.

A moment's perusal told her that something was amiss. "Surely this must be some sort of jest," she whispered, gazing in amazement at the first page. As the title registered in her mind, she snapped the book shut. This was not the story she had expected to find. It did not appear to be a novel by Mrs. Ann Radcliffe or any other writer. No, if she was not mistaken, she held in her trembling hands a book of magic!

For several moments Mary sat staring at the book, questions tumbling one after another through her mind. Who could have sent it to her? What bookseller kept such a thing in his stock? Why would anyone choose to tease her in this manner? Mary caught her breath as a more frightening thought occurred to her: if it truly were a book of magic, she must tread very carefully. The law would punish her merely for possession of such a book. That idea compelled Mary out of her bed and across her room to the fireplace, the dangerous volume clutched tightly in her hand.

Yet something more than a love of books prevented Mary from completing the action she had begun, and she stood for at least a minute staring at the fireplace, unable to consign the book to the dying embers glowing in her hearth. In the year since she had discovered them, novels had taught Mary to long for a life of excitement and adventure. Perhaps the arrival of this mysterious book signaled that her life might now veer from its otherwise dull and predictable path. With something akin to hope blossoming inside her, Mary brought the book to her wardrobe and hid it in a secret compartment, tucking it safely alongside her other treasures. Then she climbed back into bed where she passed a fitful night.

CHAPTER II

As soon as Mary's eyes fluttered open the next morning, she remembered the shock of the evening before. Now, bathed as she was in the morning sunlight, she could not help but wonder if it had been a fancy-born dream. With a nervous laugh, she said, "There probably is no book at all hidden in the wardrobe, much less a book of *magic*." She got resolutely out of her bed, crossed over to the wardrobe, and opened it. As her fingers searched the wardrobe's recesses, they brushed the book's worn cover, and her heart began to pound. She retrieved the book and gingerly opened the cover.

An Introductory Guide to the Sorcerer's Craft: a Brief History and Simple Spells for the Novice, written by Mr. A. H., proclaimed the title page.

She had not dreamt it. Within Mary a great battle began between curiosity and fear—she longed to continue reading, but was terrified of the consequences of discovery. Fright won, as with a sigh, Mary returned the book to its hiding place. Mind still filled with questions, she readied herself to break her fast with her family before hurrying downstairs.

"Mary! You look dreadful," cried Mrs. Bennet upon Mary's entrance. "Did Hill not help you dress your hair this morning?"

"No, Mama," Kitty said. "She was helping me."

"It makes no difference to me," Mary replied, relieved that she would not have to explain her pallor. "Kitty has more claim to Hill's talents than I do. What need have I for perfectly formed curls or extravagantly tied ribbons? Mine is a life of the mind, and therefore I require no external adornment."

"Indeed," replied Mrs. Bennet, turning back to Kitty to resume their conversation. "Lady Lucas assures me that the new vicar is highly qualified for his post and that he is a most handsome young man," she said. "Apparently he is the great-nephew of a *baronet*! And he brings his own fortune of ten thousand pounds a year, inherited, I believe, from his paternal grandmother. Unlike Mr. Collins." She shook her head darkly. "I will never forgive Charlotte Lucas for stealing Mr. Collins away from my girls. Surely he could have settled on Mary when Elizabeth refused him! Then Longbourn would have remained in the family. But for that horrid entail!"

"My dear Mrs. Bennet, begrudging Charlotte Lucas what meager happiness she may have found little suits you. Mary, you would have refused Mr. Collins in any case, would you not have?"

The well-worn topic of Mr. Collins and the entail served to distract Mary momentarily from her preoccupation with the book. "I believe, Papa, that I would have refused him indeed. A vain and silly man is Mr. Collins."

"You are as unfeeling a daughter as Lizzy! At least she had the decency to marry well!"

"Is the new vicar married?" asked Kitty, a hint of impatience in her voice.

"Apparently not," Mrs. Bennet replied, and with a broad wink to Kitty, she added, "But an invitation to dine at Longbourn will be issued as soon as he arrives in Hertfordshire. The Bennets shall be the first to welcome him to the parish!"

"When will he arrive?" Kitty pounced on her mother's scheme.

"I do not know, I must confess. There was some difficulty, evidently, about securing a replacement for him in Glastonbury. Lady Lucas tells me he agreed to stay on there for another six months or so while they go about engaging a new vicar."

"What perils you must wait through, my dear," Mr. Bennet chuckled. "Six months! Goodness knows what potential brides he might encounter over the course of six full months."

"Stop teasing me, Mr. Bennet. I must think of your remaining daughters' futures. When you are gone, we shall be without a home to call our own. If I can secure good marriages for Mary and Kitty, I shall feel more comfortable about your dying."

"I suppose I should be glad," replied Mr. Bennet, "that at least one of us will be comfortable with my dying."

Mrs. Bennet gave no answer.

Mary knew that her mother would think of nothing else but making a match between the new vicar and one of her daughters, but Mary had no interest in the holy state of matrimony. After her brush with heartache, she wanted nothing more to do with men and marriage. And now she had something far more interesting to occupy her attention.

***

For the following three days Mary bent her mind toward deciding what she should do with the book. She knew that she could not turn to her family for counsel. Nor did she have any friends to consult. Certainly, there was the mystery of the book's sender to solve. She had, after all, ordered it from a well-respected bookseller in London. A few explanations offered themselves to her. On the one hand, the book's arrival may have been the result of a mistake originating from the bookseller's clerk. The other hand proved far more enticing. Perhaps some mysterious benefactor had *meant* for her to receive it! Mary hoped with all of her heart that this might be true, for what could be more exciting than a secret benefactor introducing her to the world of *magic*? Many were the tales of Merlin and Morgan Le Fay that she had read, and many were the times that she had wished she could enter their world. Now, perhaps, that wish might come true. After breakfast on the third day since receiving the book, she finally resolved to open it as soon as she could return to her room.

An extended visit from Sir William and Lady Lucas thwarted Mary's plan almost immediately after it had been formulated. They had come to announce the happy news of their first grandchild's arrival into the world. Mrs. Collins fared well, they were pleased to report, and the child gave her great joy. Apparently

Lady Catherine de Bourgh had already paid the child the compliment of her well wishes. Congratulations from the Bennets were given with varying levels of sincerity—Mr. Bennet seeming genuinely pleased, Mrs. Bennet appearing less so.

When the Lucases finally departed to share their tidings in other quarters of the neighborhood, Mary attempted a retreat, but was stopped by her mother, who, agitated by the news, required an audience for her declarations of betrayal. "Not only will Charlotte Lucas become mistress of Longbourn, displacing us forever from our home," she lamented, "but she has also now provided an heir. It is hopeless!"

And so Mary's day passed in an agony of anticipation, her thoughts returning at regular intervals to the hidden compartment in her wardrobe. At long last, however, the sun set, the clock chimed, and Mrs. Bennet, spent from the day's emotions, sent her daughters to their rest before retiring herself. A storm blew outside Mary's windows, occasionally rattling the casements, but otherwise Longbourn was silent. With candle lit and door secured, Mary took the book from the wardrobe and climbed into bed. Her heart pounded as, with trembling fingers, she opened it. She lingered over the title page for only a moment before turning to the Preface and reading:

> *Magic has had a long and troubled history in Europe, nowhere more so than in the British Isles. For centuries, under the shadow of fear, sorcerers have been forced to practice their craft in secret, often hidden away in woodlands or ancient ruins. Even today, sorcerers must exercise great caution lest they be found and punished. Yet the first British*

sorcerers, a small group of peaceful men and women living in the green hills of Wales, knew no such fear. Theirs was a simple magic, mostly confined to domestic concerns. Among these people were accomplished healers of body and soul, breeders of mystical animals, and brewers of the powerful Ale of Delirium. It is from their discoveries that magic as we—

A sharp noise from down the hall startled Mary into shutting the book and blowing out her candle. Despite the silence that once again fell over the house, she drew the covers over herself and lay in the dark, glowing with excitement.

***

After that first night, Mary was impatient to retire to her room every evening. Before long she began to believe that she had found a true calling; magic, she thought, might allow her to demonstrate both taste and genius. She even felt in Mr. A. H. a kindred spirit, for his devotion to the art—and she was pleased to learn he considered it so—declared itself on every page. The obvious care and authority with which he approached the subject appealed to her.

She did admit some disappointment when she came to Mr. A. H.'s views on the casting of spells. Apparently a great believer in ease of practice, he had translated all spells of foreign origin into English. Her dissatisfaction, caused by her youthful romanticism, was only slightly alleviated by his persuasive, if somewhat blunt, argument:

There are two schools of thought regarding the language one uses to cast a spell. On the one side are the purists who endeavor to preserve the ancient traditions of magic. Adherents to this school believe that for a spell to be effective, one must always cast it in its original tongue, regardless of one's native language. While there may be some comfort in preserving tradition and establishing a connection to one's magical ancestors, I find this position otherwise ridiculous. It is nonsense to believe that for a spell to work, the sorcerer must employ foreign or long dead languages or try to wrap one's tongue around Welsh. (Of course if one is Welsh, using the language of a Welsh spell's original casting makes perfect sense.) Magic is a living, breathing entity, and should not be trapped in a dead or barely understood language. In any case, only a fraction of the magic resides in the words. The greater part stems from the intention, concentration, and will of the sorcerer, which produces mental strain enough without the added burden of remembering difficult pronunciations. In fact, one might argue that English sorcerers who use Latin or Old French do so more to win undeserved recognition than to follow tradition.

Mary felt a burning sensation creeping across her cheeks upon reading the final sentence. Too many times had she spoken about her reading or sat too long at the *pianoforte* merely to acquire attention and accolades. Feeling ashamed by this forced awareness of her conduct, she vowed to approach magic with an open heart and true humility.

Anxious to apply herself at once, she resumed reading and soon reached the introduction's final pages where, to Mary's further chagrin, she discovered that she could not immediately begin casting spells.

> *Successful magic demands absolute concentration. Consequently, before learning to cast even the simplest of spells, one must develop strong meditative abilities. Indeed, the true sorcerer can sit for hours in silent contemplation, creating vast stores of energy in order to perform magic of great complexity. Countries in the Far East, such as India, where meditation is encouraged, produce some of the finest sorcerers in the world. But this is not a skill that can be developed quickly. Therefore, I encourage the reader to exercise patience and spend time daily in practice. Although at first one may experience frustration, rest assured that there is a purpose. With a solid foundation of meditative skills, the developing sorcerer will later progress much more satisfactorily.*
>
> *The novice should begin with a simple exercise, such as watching a candle flame while allowing the mind to quiet for just a short period. Eventually both complexity and duration of the task should increase. For additional instruction, see Chapter Twelve: Exercises to Enhance Magical Skill.*

Mary set the book on her bed and looked at the candle sitting next to her on the table. Drawing a great breath, she turned all of her attention to the flame, watching as it danced in the faint draft blowing in her room. She was glad that no one could see her, for she felt quite silly. Soon enough the feeling subsided, yet her mind refused to quiet. In fact, the longer she sat in this attitude, the louder her thoughts grew, until finally she reprimanded herself for her inability to concentrate. The thoughts subsided, and for a moment, Mary knew complete peace of mind. She enjoyed the sensation, but then a worry about sustaining it crossed her mind, and the internal chatter began again. With a sigh, Mary extinguished the candle and climbed into bed.

***

Another fortnight saw Mary meditating in her room every evening, gradually achieving longer and longer periods of calm. Once she realized that meditating bore a distinct resemblance to reading in the midst of her family's chaos, her concentration improved markedly. She came to anticipate her nightly meditation with great pleasure, and when one evening the clock on her mantel told her that she had sat in silent contemplation for more than two hours, she decided she was ready to begin casting spells.

CHAPTER III

$\mathcal{A}$fter a protracted deliberation over the possibilities, Mary chose for her first spell one designed to move small objects without the necessity of touch. According to the author's instructions, the spell required only three steps:

> *First the sorcerer must place his full attention on the object to be moved. Next the destination must be determined. Finally, the sorcerer must see in his mind's eye the entire path of the object from its first position to its destination. The incantation is simple: "Move here, please," and may be spoken aloud or to oneself.*

Mary, thinking the spell's instructions absurdly easy, was convinced that she would master it with no trouble. Yet her first efforts at moving a quill across her writing desk yielded only failure. She performed the first two tasks easily enough, but imagining each detail of the quill's journey from one end of her desk to the other caused her no end of consternation. After several unsuccessful attempts left her fatigued and disheartened, Mary returned the book to its hiding place and retired for the evening.

Despite her disappointment and wounded pride, Mary slept well, awakening the next morning with renewed hope. Two more evenings passed before hope became accomplishment and the stubborn quill finally responded to her command. As she watched it roll across her desk, Mary clapped both hands to her mouth to prevent the triumphant cry from escaping. She tried again and, much to her delight, succeeded. Three more rounds proved that she had mastered the spell. That night the thrill of accomplishment overpowered her fatigue, and Mary found sleep elusive. Instead, she lay in her bed imagining what she might do with her burgeoning abilities. She settled on experimenting with the spell during tea the following day, and giggling at the prospect, chose for the object of her practice her mother's teacup.

***

"Thank you, Sarah," said Mrs. Bennet as the maid finished serving tea. After Sarah had curtsied and left the drawing room, Mrs. Bennet picked up her tea, took a delicate sip, and then set the blue and white porcelain cup and saucer on the table. With a satisfied sigh, she resumed her needlework. Mary waited until she could be certain that her mother's attention was fixed on the work in front of her before causing the cup to slide several inches back on the table. Elation coursed through her upon her success. Impatient for her mother's reaction, she nevertheless turned her head back to her book, peering surreptitiously over her glasses every few moments.

"Kitty," said Mrs. Bennet without looking up, "have you finished trimming your new bonnet with the blue ribbons?"

"Yes, Mama," replied Kitty. "Here it is," she said, holding up the newly trimmed bonnet.

"Lovely, my dear. You may wear it in the morning for our visits."

"Yes, Mama," Kitty repeated.

Setting her work in her lap, Mrs. Bennet turned to the table for her tea. "Oh," she cried, a furrow appearing in her brow.

"What is it my dear?" enquired her husband.

"Oh, not a thing, not a thing," she replied hastily. "I thought—but it is not possible."

Mary, pretending to be absorbed by her book, clenched her teeth against the giggle that threatened to erupt.

Mrs. Bennet laughed nervously and picked up her tea, sipping it daintily before returning it with precision to the table. Again Mary made it slide backwards.

"I had a letter from Jane this morning, Mr. Bennet," continued Mrs. Bennet, unaware of her teacup's wandering.

"Indeed?" came the reply from behind a newspaper. "And what is the news from Jane?"

"Everyone is well. The children had a mild influenza, but have recovered completely. Kitty, she mentioned you in particular. She said she hopes that you are enjoying your stay with us, and she looks forward to your return to Derbyshire. It seems—" But Mrs. Bennet did not complete her sentence; upon reaching again for her tea, she saw once more that it was not where she had left it.

"Yes, my dear? You were saying?" said Mr. Bennet, lowering his paper.

"What? Oh, yes. It seems that Lizzy and Mr. Darcy will be spending the season in London this year." Mrs. Bennet sipped her tea, then carefully set the teacup down. Instead of returning to her needlework, she stared at the cup. It did not move. She picked it up, took another sip of tea, and placed it back on the table. Her countenance expressing anxiety, she watched the cup for several moments more, but when it failed to move again, her face relaxed, and she resumed both work and speech. "Jane and Mr. Bingley will be joining the Darcys in London a few weeks later, she writes. But she makes no mention of Lydia and dear Mr. Wickham."

"I should think not," said Mr. Bennet. "Dear Mr. Wickham, indeed," he muttered. "The man is the biggest bl—"

A shriek from Mrs. Bennet interrupted Mr. Bennet. "Who keeps moving my tea? This is not an amusing joke! My nerves cannot stand such teasing!" cried Mrs. Bennet.

"What do you mean, my dear?" said Mr. Bennet, a hint of concern in his voice.

"Someone is playing a very nasty trick on me, and I want to know which of you is the culprit. Every time I set my tea down, it moves a little farther out of my reach," she complained, pointing an accusing finger at the delicate porcelain cup.

"My dear, are you sure that you are not setting it down farther away than you think?"

"Mr. Bennet! I know where I put my tea! I have

tea every afternoon, and every afternoon I place it very carefully within my reach when I set it down to pick up my needlework. I am not setting it farther away than I think, and I wish you would not make veiled accusations like that," snapped Mrs. Bennet. With her final word she stood and swept from the room. After a moment of stunned silence, Kitty followed, hurrying to catch up with her mother.

Mr. Bennet continued to stare in the direction taken by his wife and daughter while Mary pressed her hand to her mouth, attempting to suppress the laughter that had been threatening to escape for the duration of tea. Her efforts proved unsuccessful. The sound attracted Mr. Bennet's attention, and Mary tried to mask her amusement with a cough. A smile played on Mr. Bennet's lips, as with raised eyebrows he studied Mary closely.

"I wonder, Mary, if anyone could shed some light on this mystery."

"I imagine, Papa," said Mary, "that you are correct. Mama, her attention divided between her work and the letter from Jane, simply forgot where she set her tea."

Mr. Bennet's only reply was a slow nod. He continued to examine Mary, who, suddenly fatigued from her efforts, could not help but yawn.

"Perhaps you should take a nap," Mr. Bennet suggested.

"Indeed, Papa," said Mary. "I believe I should like to rest before dinner." And, satisfied with her experiment, she retired to her room, intent upon learning another spell.

***

After a month of diligent practice, Mary had learned all of the spells described in *An Introductory Guide to the Sorcerer's Craft*. In addition to moving small objects without touching them, she could also float feathers and other things of comparable lightness, locate lost items, disguise small objects with an effective glamour, and make light without a candle. She turned next to the study of potions, the first to catch her eye being an elixir to inspire love. Mary found Mr. A. H.'s description irresistible:

> *Love potions are surprisingly simple to make, requiring only flowers, water, and time. While roses, especially red, make fragrant and delicate love potions, the most effective flower for achieving complete domination of the will is the wild pansy, found in woodlands and meadows throughout England. It is none other than a wild pansy—what Shakespeare named "love-in-idleness"—that Oberon and Puck use with such success to cast love spells on Titania, Demetrius, and Lysander in that delightful idyll, "A Midsummer Night's Dream." Students of history or literature may be surprised to discover that Mr. Shakespeare did not devise this love spell solely from his imagination. Instead the idea came to him when he happened upon a coven in Stratford-upon-Avon gathering the flowers in the woods. He followed them to a clearing in the forest of Arden where he witnessed them brewing the potion over an open fire. The exigencies of the stage required him to compress the process, so he eliminated the brewing. Instead his characters merely crush the flower, squeezing its juice directly into their victims' eyes. For less effective love spells, the juice alone will*

suffice, resulting in nothing more than a passing fancy that will dissipate of its own accord. To create a truly binding potion you must steep the flower overnight. A few drops will achieve your desired effect; leftover potion will keep for several months if stored in a glass bottle and left in a cool, dark place. The antidote to this potion is a combination of dandelion and lavender, also steeped over night. Both potion and antidote may be taken in any form, but it is most effective and most easily administered when added to other beverages.

Mary first considered testing the potion on Maria Lucas, Charlotte Collins's younger sister, but she rejected this idea as too inconvenient—she could not watch its effects as closely as she would like. Instead she settled on her sister Kitty, who despite some marked improvement in her overall manner attributable to Jane and Elizabeth's influence, still persisted in teasing Mary more often than was strictly necessary.

The following day, rather than accompanying her mother and Kitty on their visits to neighbors and shops in the village, Mary passed a lovely morning outside, gathering pansies, dandelions, and lavender. Wisely, she had chosen to follow Mr. A. H.'s advice regarding the antidote: *Brewing both love potion and antidote at the same time is always sound practice.*

Upon her return she went immediately to her room, where she rang for Sarah and requested hot water.

"For tea?" Sarah asked. "I would be happy to make it for you, miss."

"No thank you, Sarah. You may keep the tea and

the hot water separate if you please. I have been reading about tea from the Far East, and I would like to conduct a few experiments. In fact, could you bring me two pots? I believe that will aid me in my endeavors," she said, hoping that Sarah would believe this explanation for her request.

Whatever Sarah made of her mistress's instructions, she did not say. Instead she curtsied and hurried back to the kitchen. About quarter of an hour later, Sarah returned with the requested items.

"Thank you, Sarah. That will be all," Mary said.

Again the girl curtsied and left the room.

Mary waited until she heard the maid's footsteps recede down the hallway. Then she put aside the tea leaves for use later, before placing pansies in one pot and dandelions and lavender in the other. Happily Sarah had filled both pots with hot water enough for Mary's purpose. Taking care not to spill a drop, Mary hid them in her wardrobe to steep.

In the morning Mary put a few drops of the love potion into a small glass bottle and brought it downstairs hidden in her pocket. When she arrived in the breakfast parlor, she found Kitty and Mr. Bennet seated at the table. Relieved that Mrs. Bennet had not yet arrived, Mary joined the others. Kitty sat examining some new ribbons, and Mr. Bennet had buried himself in a book. To divert Kitty's attention long enough to administer the love potion to her tea, Mary caused the ribbons to slide off the table and onto the floor.

"La, where have my ribbons gone?" Kitty exclaimed.

"I think they have fallen under the table," replied Mary.

As Kitty bent down to retrieve her ribbons, Mary poured the love potion into her sister's tea. No one noticed.

"I wonder what caused them to fall," said Kitty, sitting up. "They were so firmly set on the table. Oh never mind! Won't they make a lovely addition to my new gown? A certain Captain P. might like them." She giggled, a light pink blush blooming on her cheeks.

"Please do not be any more ridiculous than you have to be, Kitty," Mr. Bennet said. "Soldiers care not a fig for ribbons. They rarely even notice them."

"But Papa, Mr. Wickham always remarked upon the smartness of my ribbons," pouted Kitty, who, under the corrupting influence of her mother, had begun reverting to her former self.

"Mr. Wickham married Lydia. That should be proof enough for you that he lacks sound judgment."

"Really, Mr. Bennet," said Mrs. Bennet from the doorway. "To hear you speak so, one might assume that you do not care for your liveliest daughter." She entered the room. "Of course," she continued, taking her place at the breakfast table, "Jane and Elizabeth did make better *marriages*, but Lydia's husband is the most *dashing*."

Mr. Bennet returned to his reading without favoring his wife with a response. As he had oft repeated, he had learned early in his marriage that reason and truth affected his wife not at all and had ceased trying to apply them years ago. During Mrs. Bennet's chiding neither he nor his wife noticed that Kitty had stopped stroking her ribbons and chattering. Only Mary observed that her younger sister sat stone still, staring out the window. Mary followed Kitty's gaze, which rested on George, the old gardener, who was hard at work trimming the azaleas. Mary clapped her hand over her mouth as Kitty let out a sigh and continued to watch the gardener whose stooped back and bald head badly concealed by his cap ordinarily made her frown. But as the love potion took effect, Kitty wore a soft and wistful expression.

"George," she whispered.

"What did you say, Kitty?" asked her mother.

"George is outside trimming the azaleas. Does he not look handsome this morning? I do not think I have ever paid him much notice before. But after a long absence from one's home, I suppose many things change. One is granted a new perspective." Suddenly she jumped out of her seat, proclaiming, "I think I shall bring him some tea." And before the rest of her family could comprehend the meaning of her actions, Kitty had poured a cup of tea and was carrying it, a bit unsteadily, to the gardener.

Mary bit her lip to keep herself from laughing at the confused look on the old gardener's face. The family could not help but overhear their conversation through the open window.

"I brought you some tea, George," Kitty said breathlessly. "It is lovely and sweet. Here, go ahead and drink it."

With not a little trepidation, George took the cup and saucer from Kitty. He stared at it for a moment, clearly torn between his desire for the tea and his suspicion of Kitty's motives for bringing it to him. Thirst prevailed and he sipped the tea.

"Thank you, Miss Catherine," he said, still unsure about this turn of events. "This is lovely tea."

"You looked as though you might need some," Kitty said, her words tumbling one after another. "Come. Sit in the shade and rest. The sun is so hot, and I wish you to be comfortable."

"But Miss Catherine, I have work that must be done this morning."

"Go on then, I shall just sit here and watch. I love to watch you work because," Kitty said, blushing, "you are the handsomest man in the county. And— and I love you, George!"

Mary felt a moment's pity for poor, bewildered George. The gardener looked back toward the house as though seeking aid, but not finding any in that quarter, he retrieved his pruning shears and backed away, his expression betraying the belief that he was the subject of much amusement. Mary and her parents witnessed the entire exchange—Mary, lips pressed together and shaking with unvoiced laughter; Mrs. Bennet, mouth opened in confusion; and Mr. Bennet, brow furrowed in consternation.

***

For the following two days, Mary allowed the potion its continued dominance over Kitty's wit, keeping a careful eye on her sister all the while. She even made a habit of carrying the antidote in her pocket. During that short period, Mary observed as Kitty waylaid a hardworking George on several occasions, her protestations of love growing ever more insistent. On the third day, however, Mary found a sobbing Kitty prostrate at George's feet.

"Why will you not love me, George?" she asked between sobs. "I love you with all of my heart and my soul." As George once more backed away from her grasping hands, she stood, her face streaked with tears. Desperation shone in her eyes, shocking Mary, as Kitty proclaimed to the gardener's receding figure, "If you cannot love me, I shall have to drown myself or put a dagger through my heart."

That dire protestation confirmed to Mary that she had let the potion run beyond a sensible course. She cringed, recalling Mr. A. H.'s warning about the dangers of love potions:

> *Love is one of the most delicate and mysterious of the human emotions. With very little impetus it can grow from a sweet passion into a dangerous, even deadly, obsession. The subject may be overcome by his or her feelings and begin to believe that life without the object of love has extended beyond its worth. Should that or any similar sentiment be expressed, the antidote must be given as soon as possible.*

Mary hurried after her distraught sister, reaching Kitty after she had collapsed on a bench in the garden. Approaching slowly, she called, "Kitty?"

Kitty looked up, tears streaking her face. "George does not love me. I cannot go on living without him."

"Oh, my dear sister," Mary began, "it is not as bad as that. Come inside with me. We shall ask Sarah to bring us some refreshments." As she spoke she reached into her pocket and clasped the small bottle containing the antidote. Reassured by its presence, she placed her arm carefully around Kitty and helped her to her feet. "There, there, Kitty," said Mary, patting Kitty gently on the arm. "After a good cry and a cup of tea, you shall feel much better, I can assure you."

Once inside the house, Mary directed them both to Kitty's room where she summoned the maid. "Sarah, Miss Catherine has taken cold from sitting too long in the garden. Would you be so kind as to bring us tea and some cakes?"

"Of course, Miss Mary," replied Sarah before scurrying off toward the kitchens.

Mary sat next to Kitty, who had thrown herself onto the bed the moment Sarah had left. Gingerly, she stroked Kitty's hair while the poor girl indulged her broken heart. *Goodness me*, Mary thought to herself. *I must be more careful in the future. This is too severe a punishment for Kitty's teasing.*

Sarah returned with the tea, and Mary dismissed her, saying, "Thank you for your pains, Sarah." The maid curtsied and left the sisters alone.

Mary poured two cups of tea, slipping some antidote into one of them and bringing it to her sister. "Sit up now, my dear, and have a cup of tea," said Mary.

Kitty obeyed, taking the tea and sipping it absently. So distracted by the pangs of her unrequited love was she that she failed to taste the bitterness of the dandelion root, which, according to Mr. A. H., is rendered ineffective by honey or sugar.

> *It is the bitterness that makes the antidote work so effectively. The lavender provides some relief from the dandelion's flavor but is primarily added for its calming properties.*

The two sisters drank their tea in silence, Mary

carefully examining Kitty for evidence of its effect. After Kitty had finished her tea, Mary asked her, "How are you feeling now?"

"Why ever do you ask? Of course I am fine. I have a new bonnet and gown for the next ball at the Assemblies. How else should I feel?" came the indignant answer. "Why are we in my room?"

"You went for too long a walk this morning and felt a little faint. I had Sarah bring us some tea."

"Well," Kitty began, "thank you, Mary. How very kind of you." She paused. "Did—did I tell George that I love him?" she said, eyes wide with mortification.

"I do not believe you did," said Mary. "Perhaps you had a strange dream."

Kitty, soothed by the explanation, nodded. "Of course. It must have been a dream. Curious and terrible!"

Mary said nothing, but she nodded her agreement, happy that Kitty had escaped the grip of her dangerous love. She considered her experiment only partially successful, and in the future she would think twice about playing with love potions.

CHAPTER IV

*S*everal days passed in perfect safety for Mary's family, as after the love potion, she had decided it best to leave them in peace. In addition to her mounting concern for their welfare, she had begun to wonder if she had been observed. Her father seemed to be paying her more attention than he ever had before, and while she did not truly believe that he knew anything about sorcery, she chose to continue her efforts in the privacy of her room.

One morning after a night spent laboring over a complicated potion for clearing the skin, Mary came down to breakfast and discovered a letter addressed to her lying on the table. Recognizing the hand as that of her elder sister Elizabeth, she smiled and broke the seal.

Dearest Mary,

Although your preference for a quiet country life is well known to me, I hope that I may convince you of the pleasures both intellectual and musical afforded by a larger social sphere. I cannot help but think that you have grown tired of the limits attending your self-imposed exile, and I write, therefore, to extend an invitation for you to join Mr. Darcy and me in Grosvenor Square, where we intend to pass the entire season. I promise you many opportunities to demonstrate your various accomplishments.

Your most affectionate sister,

Elizabeth

Mary read the letter again, astonished both by its contents and its timely arrival. While her relationship with Elizabeth had always been cordial—indeed, she felt a great deal of admiration for her older sister—she had never considered it particularly intimate. Yet here was proof that perhaps she had underestimated Elizabeth's esteem of her—an invitation to spend the entire season in London! Nothing could have suited her better, for although Elizabeth was correct in her assumptions that Mary preferred to avoid the noise and confusion of town, after the fateful book's arrival, Mary's desires had undergone marked changes. Mary longed to pursue her magical studies further, and having finished Mr. A. H.'s *Introductory Guide*, she believed an extended stay in London would provide a means to that end.

"Is that a letter, Mary?" asked Mrs. Bennet, newly arrived for breakfast.

"Yes, Mama. Lizzy has invited me to visit her in London."

"I suppose you shall be disappointing your sister,

will you not?" Mrs. Bennet said.

"No," replied Mary. "I think I would rather like to visit Lizzy and Mr. Darcy."

"Indeed?" came Mrs. Bennet's surprised reply. "But you detest noise and crowds! Whatever could have changed your mind?"

"My dear, leave the poor child alone," rejoined Mr. Bennet from behind his newspaper. "If she wishes to go to London in the care of her sister and Mr. Darcy, why must we question her? Mary, of course you may go," he said, looking at Mary around his paper.

"Mr. Darcy's carriage has room enough for all of us," said Kitty, who was already expected in London. If Kitty felt in any way slighted by Mary's inclusion in the London journey, she did not express it.

Before the end of breakfast all was settled—Mary and Kitty would join the Darcys in London.

All afternoon and into the evening Mary wondered about the timely arrival of her sister's letter. To what did she owe the felicitous harmony it represented? Was it merely a coincidence or was it, as Mr. A. H. might suggest, *a magical convergence of events such as surround the most powerful of sorcerers?* Whatever the reason, Mary was profoundly grateful for the invitation and the possibilities it represented.

She passed the week in happy anticipation of her journey, each evening pouring over the chapters in Mr. A. H.'s guide concerned with practical matters for the novice sorcerer. The first chapter included a helpful list of shops in London where she could purchase more books to aid her study, recommending one in particular called Hartbustle and Son. According to Mr. A. H., *The current proprietor has a vast store of knowledge and an impressive collection of magical works, which makes the journey to Bloomsbury entirely worth one's while.* Mary made a note of its location, hoping that Mr. Darcy's library could provide her with a map of London.

Mary read the next chapter, entitled "Covens of England," with great excitement, for she had not even considered the existence of magical fellowships to which she might belong. She was disheartened to learn that the nearest coven to Longbourn was located outside of Cambridge. It might as well have been in Wales, she thought sadly. But her spirits were revived by the next paragraph:

> *The Bloomsbury Coven is one of the most powerful and noble magical assemblies in all of England, perhaps in all of Europe. To gain membership, hopeful sorcerers and sorceresses must prove their worth by performing magic of the most advanced— and frequently dangerous—sort. Together the members of this coven work secretly, always striving to better the condition of mankind. So earnestly do they pursue the greater good that they remove and punish any members discovered to be acting solely for their own gain. In recent years there have been no expulsions, but in the late sixteenth century, Christopher Marlowe, their most notable and notorious member, was banished from their numbers for his frequent use of magic in the staging of his plays. Afraid of discovery and punishment, the Coven had no choice but to revoke his membership. (His death in a duel shortly after his banishment is not believed to be related.)*

Mary closed the book and imagined how her life

would change if she could join this most illustrious gathering of sorcerers. She vowed to make her way to Bloomsbury at least once during her stay in London.

***

At long last the week ended, and as another week began, Mary found herself sharing Mr. Darcy's carriage with Kitty and Elizabeth. After an initial shyness she was pleased to discover an unaccustomed ease in Elizabeth's presence. In the past, envy of Elizabeth's quick wit and amiable manner had led Mary to develop an insufferable manner. From an early age, she had taken to discoursing at length about her reading. Once engaged in a lecture, she felt compelled to continue speaking, despite the obvious discomfort she detected in those forced to listen. Mary's embarrassment exceeded that of her unfortunate audience, which, to everyone's dismay, prompted further displays from the poor girl. Yet since Mary's discovery of her talent for magic, she no longer felt the pain of her insufficiencies. She had grown quieter in the weeks since the book's arrival, and in the carriage she was content to sit in silence, admiring the passing countryside and listening to her sisters talk of the months that had passed while Kitty visited Longbourn.

During a brief stop at an inn to take a small meal and to water the horses, Mary's contented contemplation was interrupted by Elizabeth's affectionate attention.

"My dear sister, you are looking very well!" said Elizabeth. "It seems an age has passed since last we met. Tell me, how have you been occupying yourself?"

Mary's reply surprised even herself with its warmth and simplicity. "Dearest Lizzy," she said, clasping her sister's hand. "I have my books, of course. They bring me to worlds I had never imagined. How can I be anything but satisfied?" She smiled and continued, "But how your eyes shine! How happy *you* appear! Matrimony suits you, does it not?"

Elizabeth raised her eyebrows as though surprised by Mary's answer. But she made no teasing comment about Mary's unusual manner, expressing instead sentiments of a different nature. "I have long wondered about your happiness, but now it gives me joy to see you have found felicity at last, Mary."

"Indeed, Lizzy, I believe I have grown a great deal happier in recent weeks," replied Mary, discovering that she spoke the truth. "I imagine we have both found felicity," she teased.

"Marriage has its pleasures," Elizabeth replied with a smile.

As they resumed their seats in the carriage, Mary reflected upon her conversation with her sister. She was moved by Elizabeth's warmth and candor and truly pleased by her sister's contentment. But once the carriage began to move, her thoughts turned toward what lay ahead. Although she endeavored to maintain a calm exterior during the journey's remainder, as they approached London's environs, Mary grew nearly breathless with anticipation of the wonders that awaited her.

The wonders were obliged to wait a little longer, for as Mary soon discovered, Elizabeth had already arranged a number of entertainments that would render any immediate exploration beyond Grosvenor Square impossible. The evening following their arrival, Elizabeth and Mr. Darcy held a ball honoring the young Miss Bennets. The invitations had been issued as soon as Mary had accepted Elizabeth's offer, and, apparently, many of London society's most distinguished members planned to attend. This information drew a sigh from Mary, which went largely unnoticed because of Kitty's more pleasurable response.

On the evening of the ball, fashionable couples arrived, and soon the ballroom was a sea of elegant gowns ornamented with beautiful jewels. Kitty, wearing a blue dress adorned with pale pink ribbons, spent a rapturous evening, never lacking a dancing partner. Mary was pleased to see that back under the careful eye of Elizabeth, Kitty's manners had improved markedly, her usual flirtation replaced with more modest conduct.

While her younger sister danced in every set, Mary preferred to observe the festivities from the comfortable vantage of the benches judiciously placed around the ballroom. The entire scene was laid out before her, and she could not resist employing a few simple spells to amuse herself. For about a quarter of an hour, she followed the progress of a slender, rakish young man and his vain partner. She had noticed that the young woman watched Kitty with a jealous eye. When Mary overheard an unflattering remark made by the young woman to her partner concerning the quality of Kitty's gown, Mary encouraged the young man's right foot to slip from beneath him, causing him to stagger and to pull his partner off balance.

"What are you doing?" whispered the young lady

as she stumbled past Mary, grasping without grace for her partner's arm. "You are embarrassing me!"

"I certainly have no intention of causing you mortification," he whispered back. "I merely tripped. The floor must have a fault in it. Yes, that must be the explanation."

The couple danced on, heads held high as though challenging anyone to mock them. Mary giggled, pleased with herself for the subtlety of the spell. She turned her eye back to the dancers, anxious to practice another spell, but the set had ended, leading to a natural break in the dancing. Several young ladies stood in a cluster near Mary, fanning themselves after their exertions. She recognized among their number Miss Caroline Bingley, sister to Mr. Bingley, Jane's husband. Mary fixed her eyes on Miss Bingley, and the haughty young woman dropped her fan. Laughing affectedly, she bent to retrieve it. A moment later it slipped out of her fingers.

"Goodness!" she exclaimed as she stooped to pick up the fan.

Again it fell to the ground. Again Miss Bingley picked it up, her laughter acquiring a frantic quality.

"My word, Miss Bingley," said a gentleman standing nearby, witness to the events. "Are you well? Would you like some refreshment?"

"I suppose I would," replied Miss Bingley. "I seem to be having difficulty gripping my fan. It has grown so terribly slippery."

"Allow me to accompany you. We shall find some wine," said the young gallant, offering his arm, which Miss Bingley happily took. Leaving her fan behind, Miss Bingley retreated from Mary's view.

Soon enough the music began again, and the

dancers returned to the floor. It was a lively piece with intricate musical flourishes. But the set was interrupted when, after an impressive run of notes, the violinist's bow flew out of his hand, soared across the room, and landed in a potted plant. A servant happened to be passing the plant, carrying a tray laden with glasses. So startled was he that he jumped backward, knocking into a portly gentleman and dropping his tray. Both tray and glasses came down with a crash. The already confused guests searched the room for the source of the unpleasant noise. A flurry of activity followed as maids were sent to clean the mess and to retrieve the offending bow.

Mary, thinking herself unnoticed, burst into laughter. But almost immediately she stopped, certain that someone watched her. She glanced around until she saw a tall stranger staring at her from across the room. As she met his gaze, Mary saw him shake his head almost imperceptibly, and she realized with a start that the tall stranger knew that *she* had caused the confusion. Moreover, in that slight shake of his head, Mary read disappointment and disapproval. She stopped laughing, feeling a hint of shame, although unsure of its origins. She ducked her head, momentarily breaking eye contact, and when she looked back toward him, he turned and strode from the room.

Wishing to discover more about this mysterious stranger, Mary followed him out of the ballroom. His path took her into the salon where she hid behind the window's thick velvet drapes, allowing her to observe from a discreet distance as he approached her brother-in-law, Mr. Darcy. She watched the two gentlemen for a few moments, but unable to hear their conversation, she soon abandoned her post. Rather than return to the ball, she retired to her room to ponder the curious turn of events, filled with remorse for her actions. Perhaps tricks were not the best use for her talent.

***

About a week after the eventful ball, Mary finally managed to slip away from her family. She made her way to a nearby market where she had the good fortune to find a book fair under way. Upon entering the market, Mary paused and drew a great breath.

Everywhere she looked stood tables piled with books of every shape and color. She could not believe the pure beauty of this vision and the excitement coursing through her in the face of it. She stood in an attitude of awe for several minutes, having momentarily forgotten her purpose.

After she recovered herself, she stopped at the first table to examine the books and greeted the awkward young man standing behind it.

"Good afternoon," said Mary. "You have a lovely collection of books."

The young man blinked at her rapidly and stuttered his thanks. Not knowing how best to phrase an enquiry about the sort of book she hoped to find, she continued, "I am content simply to look if that pleases you."

"Yes, Miss. And if you would like to p-p-purchase any b-b-book, I am at your s-s-service."

Mary nodded and smiled at the poor, flushed young man. She took care to examine all the books on display, experiencing a momentary thrill when she saw the word *Spell* written on a book half-hidden under another. But in the next moment her heart fell when she uncovered the book and read the rest of the title, *ing Reform*. Certain that she had seen everything offered, she smiled again at the clerk and moved along.

Still filled with hope, she progressed to the next table. But it also proved disheartening. And so her morning unfolded. After several more disappointments, Mary decided to seek some refreshment. She located a stall where she could purchase a cup of tea and a roll. A few tables ringed by chairs stood nearby; Mary availed herself of one to rest and to enjoy her tea and muffin. At the table next to her sat a short, round gentleman also drinking tea. A friendly face beamed at her from under a mop of silvery white curls. He inclined his head in her direction, and she smiled in response.

Just then a young woman cried out, "My purse, he has stolen my purse!"

Mary leapt from her seat to see the culprit running by a table stacked with heavy folios. Without another thought, she sent the folios flying into the thief's path, knocking him over. To ensure his incapacitation, she caused another pile of books to tumble to the floor where they arranged themselves around him, forming a little prison. A constable was summoned, the man was led away, and the purse was returned. Feeling gratified by helping someone with her magic, Mary finished her tea and resumed her search.

Had she looked behind herself after her actions, she would have noticed that the gentleman with the silvery white curls had witnessed her part in the momentary drama. She might have recognized his bemused expression. But as she walked back toward the tables of books, she failed to feel his gaze following her.

Only further discouragement met Mary as she moved through the fair. On table after table she found books on every subject *but* magic. Her hope turned to dismay as she neared the end of the market, until she arrived at a table tended by the gentleman from the tea stall. He greeted Mary warmly.

"Good afternoon, my dear. May I be of service to you? Are you looking for anything in particular? A novel, perhaps? I have a copy of *The Mysteries of Udolpho* only slightly worn at the edges that I can sell to you for six shillings ten pence."

Mary sighed. "No thank you. I already have a copy. Today I am looking for something different, but I cannot seem to find what I would like," she replied.

As she turned to leave, the gentleman smiled at her again and said, "Please do not be downhearted, my dear, I may have what you seek." Before Mary could question his meaning, the gentleman was digging in a trunk stashed under another table heavy with books. When he stood up he held three volumes.

"Perhaps these are more to your taste."

Mary took the first book and examined it. It had a faded leather cover with no writing on the binding. Puzzled, she looked at him.

"Open the cover," he whispered.

She did as he asked. Her eyes grew large when she read the title page. *Developing Your Craft*, it said. Hurriedly she did the same with the other two books, *Magicks and Sorceries* and *Spells*.

Mary, all astonishment, stared at the man for a moment before remembering her manners and smiling.

"Thank you, sir! These *do* satisfy my tastes." Then she lowered her voice to a whisper and continued, "But how did you know I was looking for such books?"

"I share your interest in certain arts. Well done waylaying that thief," he whispered back to her. "But in the future, you should exercise more caution. Such *actions* may draw much unwanted attention."

"Again, I thank you," said Mary, blushing.

"Of course, my dear. One must always look after one's fellows! In fact, here is my card should you require further reading on the subject."

Mary took the card. *Mr. Henry Hartbustle, Hartbustle and Son, purveyors of books large and small. No manuscript too rare*, it read, giving a now familiar address in Bloomsbury.

"Oh!" cried Mary. "How fortuitous!"

"Indeed? Have you heard of my modest shop?"

"I have! It is described in *An Introductory Guide to the Sorcerer's Craft: a Brief History and Simple Spells for the Novice*," she explained.

"Ah, yes, I know it well. I hope, then, that I shall have the honor of a visit at some time in the future, Miss…?"

"Oh, yes, Mary Bennet," she replied hastily. "I should be glad to pay you a visit," she replied.

"I look forward to it with great anticipation, Miss Bennet. In the meanwhile, should you have any questions, please do not hesitate to write if you cannot spare the time to venture as far as Bloomsbury."

"Thank you, Mr. Hartbustle," said Mary with sincerity. Then she turned and left the kind bookseller at his stall.

When she returned to Mr. Darcy's townhouse, Mary found her family in the drawing room, receiving guests. Jane and Mr. Bingley were seated on the sofa drinking tea. Next to them sat Mrs. Bennet, lately arrived to spend a few weeks in London with her daughters. Kitty, Elizabeth, and Mr. Darcy occupied other chairs in the room. As Mrs. Bennet saw her daughter enter, she exclaimed, "Mary Bennet! Where in heaven's name have you been?"

"I have been out walking, Mama. I took a turn around the square and then sat in the park to read."

"Well, you should have notified someone. We have been worried sick about you."

Mary looked around at her sisters and their husbands. No one seemed to be suffering from her absence. "I am sorry, Mama. I promise never to do that again."

"Good. Now take some refreshment. You must be thirsty after your exertions."

Mary obeyed, and although she longed to return to her room to begin reading, she knew that she would have to spend a tedious hour listening to the gossip of the city. Her first thought was to practice her spells on her family, but with a blush of shame, she remembered the young man at the ball. So she attempted to follow the conversation already in progress. When she grew tired of feigning interest in the talk around her, Mary cast a subtle spell on her new books so that she could, as was her habit, read in the midst of the family. Although she now opened *Developing Your Craft*, her family, should they have bothered to look her way, would have seen *A Treatise on Sobriety and its Joys* and would leave her to read in peace.

CHAPTER V

And so the weeks in London passed—each day finding Mary advanced further toward mastery of the spells in her new books. Her daily practice of magic also had the happy effect of teaching her to manage her energy with more care. Soon the casting of simple spells no longer produced more fatigue than might a casual stroll in a well-shaded garden. Once or twice she considered writing a note to Mr. Hartbustle, but decided against arousing the suspicion such a correspondence would excite in her family. Instead she resolved to visit his shop as soon as the opportunity presented itself. She found a map of London in Mr. Darcy's library, which she studied with great interest, tracing possible courses through town. Bloomsbury was at a marked distance from Grosvenor Square, but Mary counted herself a stout walker and dismissed the distance as a problem.

As chance would have it, an opportunity presented itself one afternoon while Kitty and Mrs. Bennet shopped in Bond Street. Mary, having accepted their invitation to join them, feigned fatigue, saying, "Mama, Kitty, if it is no trouble to you, I believe I shall return home to rest. I do not have the constitution necessary to enjoy being so much abroad among all these people."

"Of course, Mary. I was surprised that you chose to accompany us. Would you like me to send for someone to attend you?" asked her mother.

"Oh, no, Mama. I believe I can find my way back to Mr. Darcy's house. Solitude suits me best."

With little more ceremony, she left Mrs. Bennet and Kitty exclaiming over some silken gloves and began the walk to Bloomsbury. On another day she might have taken time to enjoy the sights London had to offer, but not this day. Her anticipation was too great, and it drove her to adopt a quick pace.

When she finally arrived at Mr. Hartbustle's shop in Lamb's Conduit Street, she caught her breath, opened the door, and crossed the threshold. It was a bright and cheery place, situated near a lively public house called The Lamb, with wide windows that let in the afternoon light. Shelves laden with books of all shapes and sizes lined the walls from floor to ceiling. "So beautiful!" Mary whispered as her gaze wandered across the books.

"Welcome!" came the cheery voice of Mr. Hartbustle. "I am delighted to see you," he said, as he climbed nimbly down a ladder that leaned against one of the walls. In one arm he balanced several books, with the other he waved to her to join him. "I have been wondering when or if I would see the charming young lady from the market again! And here you are! Come in, come in."

She followed him through the shop, wondering at

his dexterity as he made his way through precarious stacks of books. As far as Mary could tell, only Mr. Hartbustle's white curls hinted that he was not still a young man. He stopped by a small table covered in books and flanked by two comfortable chairs, one of which was home to a very fat sleeping cat. Mary noticed an ornate wooden door nearby and wondered what lay beyond it.

"If you have time for a visit, I shall clear the table and bring wine and cake. I have been saving the last drops of a lovely bottle of Madeira for a special occasion; your visit may certainly be characterized so!"

At the sound of Mr. Hartbustle's voice, the cat awoke, stretched, and then hopped to the floor without acknowledging their presence. Mr. Hartbustle gave a delighted chuckle. "Well, my word! He has given up his favorite place in your honor. That is a rare event indeed!" he said, as he cleared the books from the table. "Now, if you will excuse me, Miss Bennet, I shall return in a moment."

He disappeared behind the ornate door, leaving Mary to gaze at her surroundings, still struck with amazement by the presence of all those books. Not even Mr. Darcy's library with its remarkable collection could compare to the wonder of Mr. Hartbustle's shop. She bent to examine the pile of books next to her chair.

"I must apologize for the mess," said Mr. Hartbustle, setting a tray on the small table. "My assistant has not been well, and I have not had time to catalogue everything yet."

"Your collection is remarkable!" exclaimed Mary. "I have never seen so many books in one place."

"My sincerest thanks, Miss Bennet," he said, as he served the cake and wine. "The shop has been in my family for several generations, so we have had ample opportunity to amass this lovely mess. But," he added, winking, "I do not suppose it was to hear a history of my family's business that brought you here today."

Mary smiled, feeling herself at ease in the glow of the gentleman's kindness. As they took their refreshments, she recounted the tale of her entry into the magical world. "Although I have wondered at length, I still have come upon no satisfactory explanation for the book's arrival," she concluded.

"Sometimes happy accidents occur," Mr. Hartbustle said, smiling at her. "We do not always need to understand the why of something. We can just appreciate that it is so."

"But what if the book was meant for someone else?"

"I cannot believe that to be the case," said Mr. Hartbustle. "And even if it were, you have made it yours by mastering its contents."

For some reason Mary's thoughts turned to the spells she had performed at the ball and the mysterious young man's obvious disapproval. She considered sharing the incident with Mr. Hartbustle, but embarrassment prevented her. Instead she asked, "Have you been—I am not certain I quite know how to say it—"

"A sorcerer?"

"Yes! Have you been one all your life?"

"I suppose I have been, although it was hardly my primary pursuit. From a young age I assisted my father in this bookshop. My mother died when I was but an infant, so my father, bereft of her company and aid, enlisted me to perform little tasks as he went about the more complicated business of selling books. We spent most of our time here or in the rooms above the shop where I still live, alone now that my father has gone to his rest."

"How did you come to realize what you are?"

"My father counted himself a friend to the magically inclined and kept a small inventory of *interesting* texts. When I was just a boy, I discovered them. He did not discourage me from learning, but he did extract a vow of extreme care to keep me safe from any persecution should I develop into a sorcerer of any note. So, you see," he said, eyes twinkling, "we have much in common. Like you, I learned most of what I know from books."

"Most?" Mary prompted, her interest piqued.

"Indeed, my dear. You see, no book, no matter how clearly written, can make one into a sorcerer without a certain aptitude for the craft in the first place. And even then, it is only through careful *practice* that one's potential may be reached. Books teach us the *shape* of spells; exertion reveals their finer points."

Mary nodded, beaming.

"Ah, I seem to have hit upon something meaningful to you!"

"Oh yes! Everything seemed so simple on the page. But when I made my first attempts, I failed horribly. I had to work through the difficulties with something more than words." She stopped, confused. "I think I have left sense behind, as my father would say."

"No, no, my dear. I understand your meaning completely." He smiled. "A sorcerer's instinct, we might call it. I believe that is partially what you mean."

"Yes," said Mary. "Instinct."

From somewhere in the shop came the chime of a clock.

"Oh, my word!" cried Mary. "I must be getting home. They will have missed me by now. I am certain of it."

"Have you far to walk?"

"I am afraid I do. I am staying with my older sister and her husband in Grosvenor Square. I slipped away from my mother and younger sister while we were shopping in Bond Street."

"Do not fret, my dear!" said Mr. Hartbustle rising to his feet. He motioned for Mary to follow him. "I shall show you a simple route through London that will allow you to travel quickly and without attracting any unwanted attention."

Curious about Mr. Hartbustle's intentions, Mary obeyed. They reached the front of his store, and he turned to her. "I imagine instructions are best given here. In a moment I shall lead you to a door through which you will find a great stone corridor lined with other doors. There are also a few other pathways branching off from the main passage, but you need not worry about those. You will simply follow that passage until you come to a door labeled 'Bond Street.' If you arrive at 'St. James,' you have traveled too far. Open the door and you will find yourself in Bond Street, very close to your destination. Do you understand?"

"Yes," said Mary. "But how does it work?"

"On the principle that the shortest distance between two points is a straight line, my dear. Instead of winding your way through London, you will simple walk directly to your destination."

"Astonishing!" cried Mary. "To think that such a thing is possible!"

"It is rather remarkable when one stops to think about it," he agreed, opening the door and ushering Mary through. He stood in the open doorway and pointed at a small door a few feet away that Mary had not noticed when she had arrived earlier. "Through there, Miss Bennet," he whispered. "And turn right."

Mary nodded.

"I hope you shall find time again to visit me," Mr. Hartbustle said.

"Of course I will," replied Mary. "As soon as I can slip away!" She waved and then, filled with excitement, opened the door to enter the mysterious passage. Before closing the door she chanced to look across the street where she caught a glimpse of a familiar face. Wondering whose it might be, she closed the door and turned to walk away, until with a gasp she realized it was the young man she had seen at the ball. She pulled the door open again and searched the street in vain. He had disappeared. "How strange!" she murmured, turning back to the corridor. But the sight that unfolded before her drove all other concerns from her mind.

She stood entranced as her eyes began to adjust to the flickering light of the great stone corridor. It was a wide, enclosed avenue with doors cut into the stone every few feet. Letters of varying design and color glowed on the doors, enhancing the illumination provided by lamps set every few yards in nooks carved into the walls. Mary began walking slowly, reading the doors as she passed them. She noticed that some of the lettering was ornate, glowing with a soft golden light, whereas other doors proclaimed their destination with far more simplicity. Because she was in a hurry to return home, she began walking faster and arrived at a door labeled "Bond Street" in a few minutes.

Upon opening the door, Mary blinked in the strong sunlight. When her eyes had adjusted, she made note of the door's location so that she could find it again and return to Mr. Hartbustle's shop. With a light step Mary walked the rest of the way to Mr. Darcy's house, already planning her next journey through the magic corridor. As she neared the townhouse, her thoughts turned toward devising an excuse for her disappearance—unnecessarily as only a maid and the butler noticed her arrival. Mary hurried upstairs, wondering at her good fortune. She could now proceed as though she had spent the entire afternoon resting in her room and then with perfect innocence join the others at dinner, secure in her secret.

***

Not a full week had passed before another opportunity to visit Mr. Hartbustle presented itself. Mary arrived downstairs for breakfast and found herself dining alone. After waiting at least a quarter of an hour for anyone to join her, Mary addressed the young servant girl attending her. "Jennie, have you any idea where everyone has gone?"

"Yes, Miss Mary," replied Jennie. "Mrs. Bennet, Miss Catherine, and Mrs. Bingley have accompanied Mrs. Darcy on her morning visits, and Mr. Darcy and Mr. Bingley have retired to Mr. Darcy's club for the morning. Is there anything you need, Miss? Mrs. Darcy gave me strict instructions to look after you. 'See to it that Miss Mary is comfortable, Jennie,' she said to me just before she left."

"Thank you, Jennie. I believe I have everything I require. After breakfast I shall take a walk around the square, so you need not worry about me any longer," said Mary. She remained the picture of calm to Jennie while inwardly her thoughts raced toward the corridor of doors that would take her to the bookshop in Lamb's Conduit Street.

With no difficulty Mary located the small door in Bond Street and slipped through it into the stone passage. She shivered in the cool air and began a brisk walk toward Lamb's Conduit Street. Just past the door marked Covent Garden, she came upon a smaller path branching off from the main thoroughfare. Wondering where that might lead, she continued on, anxious to arrive in Bloomsbury.

Less than a quarter of an hour after she had left Mr. Darcy's house, Mary came to the door marked Lamb's Conduit Street in thin, silver letters. She opened it slowly, careful not to hit anyone who might be walking past, and then turned towards Mr. Hartbustle's shop. A glance into the window arrested her progress, for she saw the proprietor engaged in an animated conversation with a tall, thin woman whose pale, sharp features lent her an unhappy aspect. As Mr. Hartbustle spoke, the woman shook her head, pursing her lips and furrowing her brow. His entreaties, for that is what his gestures suggested to Mary, appeared unsuccessful. Not wishing to interrupt, Mary started to leave, intending to take a turn around the block before attempting another visit. But her movement must have caught the eyes of both parties. A knock on the window stopped Mary, who turned to see Mr. Hartbustle waving to her. She raised her hand to return his gesture when the pale woman caught her eye. Such a gaze Mary had never before experienced. The coldness in the stranger's eyes sent a chill racing through her, and, for a moment, she was frozen, unable to move. A heavy silence surrounded her, within which she could hear her breath coming in gasps and her heart beating quickly in her chest.

The mysterious spell was broken only by the appearance of Mr. Hartbustle at her side. He touched her lightly on the arm, and the sounds of the street came rushing back to her.

"My dear Miss Bennet!" he said. "How lovely to see you again. Please, join us in the shop!"

The cheer in his voice did much to warm Mary, and taking his arm, she allowed him to lead her inside. In the bookseller's merry presence, Mary could almost convince herself that she had imagined the entire episode. She remained slightly shaken, however, and not at all anxious to make the pale woman's acquaintance. An introduction, nevertheless, was precisely what Mr. Hartbustle intended.

"How felicitous that you arrived when you did, Miss Bennet! I had just this moment begun to describe you to Mrs. Post as one who shares certain of our *interests*. I explained your natural aptitude and considerable talent, you see."

"Oh?" said Mary, flushing under the attention. "Th—thank you! I am flattered by the compliment."

"Not at all, my dear. *I* should be flattered by your taking time to visit me twice in one week!"

Feeling obligated to acknowledge Mrs. Post, Mary held out her hand, saying, "I am pleased to make your acquaintance, Mrs. Post."

Mrs. Post, taking Mary's outstretched hand in her own cold one, forced a smile that did not reach her eyes and replied, "And I, yours, Miss Bennet." But the appraising look she leveled at Mary spoke of anything but pleasure.

"Mrs. Post and I belong to a small group of people who meet once a fortnight to discuss our shared interests, Miss Bennet. I was convincing her of the merits of inviting you to join us Friday for our meeting."

Mrs. Post raised an eyebrow at Mr. Hartbustle, which communicated her displeasure quite clearly.

"You shall have to excuse Mrs. Post for her caution," continued Mr. Hartbustle appearing unconcerned. "Our group must remain clandestine, as I am sure you understand. My friend worries about discovery, but I have assured her that you pose no threat to our safety. In fact, I believe you could be a tremendous addition to our numbers."

"All in good time, Mr. Hartbustle," said Mrs. Post.

Mr. Hartbustle gave an affable wave, which nonetheless dismissed Mrs. Post's response. "Perhaps I do get ahead of myself. Naturally we must count on our young friend to decide if our group can be of service to her."

Mrs. Post's expression suggested she believed something quite to the contrary, but she bowed her head in a gesture of acquiescence. Delighted, Mr. Hartbustle continued, "Miss Bennet, perhaps we can persuade Mrs. Post to remain with us for another quarter of an hour or so of pleasant conversation?"

"I am afraid not, Mr. Hartbustle," said Mrs. Post. "I have another engagement across town this morning. Think of what I said, Henry," she finished before sweeping out of the shop. She gave Mary one more cool glance, which raised the hairs on the back of Mary's neck.

Mr. Hartbustle chuckled. "I apologize for my friend," he said. "She can be somewhat abrupt at times. But she is a very wise woman and has much to teach if you would like to learn. Now tell me, my dear, how may I help you this morning?"

Mary knew she ought to feel slighted, but in Mr. Hartbustle's presence she found that impossible. His good-natured attention to her smoothed over the uncomfortable moments with Mrs. Post so that by the time Mary left the shop, she was convinced that her imagination, given to flights of fancy, had constructed it all. She carried with her two books that Mr. Hartbustle had insisted would prove useful, having finally relented to borrowing them.

"If you will not accept the books as gifts," he said, "you must at least consent to borrow them for as much time as you would like."

"Thank you, sincerely, Mr. Hartbustle," Mary replied.

"Of course my dear. And you will give some thought to my offer? May I expect you on Friday morning for our meeting?"

"I would be honored," she said, and then smiling broadly she left the shop and returned to Mr. Darcy's house.

CHAPTER VI

*M*ary passed the week between her second visit to Mr. Hartbustle and the much-anticipated Friday morning in a state of agitated excitement. Try as she might, she could not contain her feelings. As a result she was far more restless than usual. The night before she was to join Mr. Hartbustle and his friends, she could not remain for any length of time in one place, prompting her mother to observe, "Goodness, Mary! Whatever has gotten into you? You have not been still above a minute since retiring here after dinner. You are unsettling my nerves with your fidgeting!"

"I apologize, Mama. I suppose I am suffering from an excess of energy," said Mary. "Perhaps tomorrow I shall take a long walk in the park. Yes, I believe I will do that first thing in the morning." She had hit upon a wonderful excuse to be out all morning, and was congratulating herself inwardly when her clever plan was upset.

"May I join you, Mary?" said Kitty. "I think I should like a turn in the park very much."

Kitty's request left Mary speechless. How was she to sneak to Bloomsbury if her sister accompanied her on her walk? Her hesitation prompted a renewed appeal from Kitty, seconded by Mrs. Bennet.

"Oh, do walk with your sister, Mary," said Mrs. Bennet. "In fact, we could all make a morning of it."

"What a wonderful idea," said Elizabeth. "I shall accompany you, and I will send a note to Jane inviting her along," she added, retrieving her writing desk from a table in the corner.

While Elizabeth sat composing the letter to Jane and the other ladies chattered about their new morning plans, Mary labored to hide her consternation. How could she get to Mr. Hartbustle's shop if her entire family accompanied her on her imaginary walk? Her mind raced as she sought an escape from them, but to no avail. Finally Mary decided that she had no choice but to send a note to Mr. Hartbustle excusing her absence. With a heavy heart she listened to her family's animated discussion until it was time to retire for the evening.

Back in her room Mary composed her short note and then rang for a maid to post it. After the maid left with assurances that the letter would be sent immediately, Mary prepared herself for bed. Perhaps she would be invited again to attend one of Mr. Hartbustle's meetings before she left London. The idea provided sufficient cheer, which allowed sleep to come without excessive struggle.

Mary rose early the next morning and arrived in the breakfast parlor to find a small package waiting for her. Rather than risk discovery, for she hoped Mr. Hartbustle had sent the package, she returned to her room to open it in private. A small, aromatic pouch accompanied by a short note tumbled onto her bed. She tore open the letter and read:

My Dear Miss Bennet,

I believe I have a solution to the problem you outlined in your charming note. Contained within this pouch you will find a forgetfulness potion made from dried betel leaf. You need only administer a pinch to some liquid, and your family will forget that they ever intended to join you on the walk. I have modified the potion slightly by adding shaved Valerian root, which will produce a gentle lethargy of mind and body, discouraging everyone from even a slight desire to leave the house until much later in the day.

I look forward, therefore, to seeing you in my shop shortly after ten o'clock in the morning.

Your humble friend,

H. Hartbustle

A potion to erase the memory! Of course, how could she have forgotten? She had read about that potion just recently in one of her new books. Before she could berate herself much further, she realized that she would never have managed to find dried betel leaf or Valerian root without considerable trouble. Relieved, she tucked the pouch into her pocket and returned to the breakfast-parlor.

A simple distraction was all she needed to put the

potion in the teapot standing on the sideboard. As she ate her breakfast, she watched her family for signs that it had taken effect. She did not have to wait for long.

"Goodness," said her mother yawning, "I thought I had passed a good night. But I think I shall return to my room and rest."

"Were we not planning some excursion today?" Elizabeth asked, rubbing her eyes.

"I suppose we were," said Jane, "for I cannot imagine any other reason that I have joined you for breakfast. But I believe I should like nothing more than to sit quietly in the salon all morning."

Mary looked over to where Kitty sat; her sister had fallen asleep with her head resting on the table. Suppressing her joy, Mary yawned and said, "Oh my, I am quite fatigued. I suppose I should return to my bed."

No one responded, so she slipped out of the room, down the hall, and out the door. Her high spirits carried her all the way through the magical corridor to Bloomsbury.

"I see you managed to steal away after all," said Mr. Hartbustle by way of greeting.

Mary smiled brightly. "I am in your debt once again. How did you procure betel leaf? Does that not originate in the far reaches of the Orient?"

"It does indeed," he replied, returning her smile. "But it is not so difficult to locate when one knows where to look. Now, my dear, follow me. The others await your arrival with much eagerness!"

She followed Mr. Hartbustle through the shop, passing the chairs, now empty of the cat. Before Mary could comment on the cat's absence, Mr. Hartbustle had opened the ornate door and ushered her into a cozy room. In the center a table made of dark wood stood majestically on an Indian rug, rich with colors and design. Five people of varying ages and shapes sat in wooden chairs around the table, all of them looking at her.

Of the five Mary recognized only Mrs. Post, who held her face in a neutral mask, suggesting she had softened perhaps a little since the moment of their first acquaintance.

Mr. Hartbustle closed the door, saying, "Please join us at the table, Miss Bennet. I have arranged a place for you next to me, as you can see."

He waited for Mary to settle herself. Taking his seat, he continued, "Miss Bennet, it gives me great pleasure to introduce you to our little group: Mr. Edmund Spottiswoode, Mr. Michael Callan, Lady Patricia Vinton, and Miss Emilia Clarkson. Of course, you have already made Mrs. Edwina Post's acquaintance."

As they were introduced, the members of Mr. Hartbustle's group nodded toward her with varying degrees of courtesy. Mary sensed that their smiles covered shrewd judgment and felt herself blush under their scrutiny. Attempting to ignore the increasing awkwardness of her situation, Mary turned her attention to Mr. Hartbustle. But she was shocked out of her discomfort by Mr. Hartbustle's next statement.

"Together," he said, "we call ourselves the Bloomsbury Coven."

"The Bloomsbury Coven?" Mary repeated, awestruck. What luck to find herself among the most illustrious group of sorcerers in all of Britain! And yet Mary felt a shiver of trepidation run through her. She could not believe that she was worthy to sit in their presence, much less listen to their business.

"You have heard of us?" said Mr. Hartbustle, obviously pleased.

Mary composed herself to answer. "Why, yes, I—I have read about you!"

"Ah! Of course!" he smiled. "*An Introductory Guide to the Sorcerer's Craft: a Brief History and Simple Spells for the Novice*! How could I have forgotten? You told me about the book during our first visit. Written by a Mr. A. H. Wise of him not to disclose his full name—a sound choice to protect himself from persecution and prosecution."

As Mr. Hartbustle spoke, Mary thought she saw Miss Clarkson and Lady Vinton exchange a look that spoke of some significance. She could not be certain as the two women were situated at the other end of the table. Perhaps she had imagined it, she supposed when Mr. Hartbustle caught her eye. Under the influence of his kind smile, she forgot her anxiety. If Mr. Hartbustle believed she belonged there, then perhaps she did.

As the meeting was called to order, Mary straightened in her seat, filled with a sense of the moment's significance. "This morning's business," Mrs. Post began in deep yet hushed tones, "concerns that traitorous sorcerer who has plagued us with his viciousness for too long. We finally possess the information necessary to perform our duty to the world and stop him. After months of fruitless searches, I have learned that he has taken up residence in Glastonbury. We do not yet know his exact location, but with the knowledge now at our disposal, it will not be long before we can find him and eliminate him."

"Wonderful!" cried Mr. Callan.

"Most welcome news!" exclaimed Miss Clarkson, while the others nodded in agreement.

Mary held her breath. Here were far loftier uses for magic than playing paltry tricks on her family and friends or impeding petty criminals. She began to hope that the Bloomsbury Coven might extend her an invitation to join their efforts. But the hope was dashed almost immediately after it had arisen.

"My dear Mrs. Post, dear Mr. Hartbustle," chimed Lady Vinton, a plump woman of middle age dressed all in mauve with shockingly red hair arranged in elaborate curls. "I must voice my concern, once again, about engaging in this particular business while a *stranger* plays witness." She turned to Mary. "I *beg* your pardon, Miss Bennet," she said in a sweet voice. "I *hate* to call attention to you in such a stark manner, but the delicate matters we are deliberating today must never be uttered beyond these walls. Even *we* do not discuss the subjects of our meetings once we leave this room. I *do* hope you understand."

The attention leveled at her by Lady Vinton caused Mary a measure of discomfort. But the unpleasantness was tempered by the amusement she felt watching Lady Vinton's chubby hands move in such a way to call attention to the richly jeweled rings adorning her fingers. Mary was on the verge of laughter when she caught Lady Vinton's expression. The laughter died, replaced by shock at the hardness in the green eyes that met hers.

Mrs. Post, annoyance plain on her face, opened her mouth to answer, but before she could speak, Mr. Hartbustle held up his hand, saying, "My dear Lady

Vinton, can you truly believe that I would invite anyone with whom our secrets would not be safe? I vouch for Miss Bennet with full confidence."

"Of *course*. *Indeed*. So you *said*. But one cannot be *too* cautious, can one? Your unsettling notions about rank and merit notwithstanding, *Mr.* Hartbustle, who is she, this *novice* from a family of *no* significance, to share in the—"

"Lady Vinton, I do not wish to tread this ground again," said Mr. Hartbustle, a hint of iron beneath his cordial tone. He looked around the table as if challenging anyone to contradict him. When no one did, he smiled broadly and continued, "Excellent. We are all agreed. Now, Mr. Spottiswoode, I believe you had a report to make. Please feel free to proceed."

Mary's face had grown warm with shame at the aspersions cast on her family; she wondered what Lady Vinton might have said had Mr. Hartbustle allowed her to continue and cast a surreptitious glance down the table at her. The woman smiled tightly through pursed lips, but her whole being seethed. Not wishing to draw any more of Lady Vinton's attention, Mary fixed her eyes instead on the short, stout man of about fifty years to her left. He rose, cleared his throat impressively, and began speaking in a high, quavering voice not at all fitting his physique.

"I have learned through my enquiries that a ship laden with spices and tea from India vanished from the Port of London about a week ago. The ship's crew was found wandering the beach, unaware of their surroundings and suffering from starvation and thirst. Some appeared to have been beaten within an inch of their lives. All gave testimony of being overcome, but by what they could not agree." Mr.

Spottiswoode paused, eyebrows raised as though to communicate the seriousness of his message. "Moreover," he continued, prompted by a nod from Mrs. Post, "in addition to the valuable teas and spices, the ship may have carried a number of arcane volumes of Eastern magical lore. It is my suspicion—"

"I beg your pardon, Mr. Spottiswoode," said Miss Clarkson, a young woman Mary estimated to be close to her own age and therefore the youngest member of the coven.

"Yes, Miss Clarkson?" said Mr. Spottiswoode, startled by the interruption. He blinked several times and looked toward Mrs. Post who pursed her lips and gave an almost imperceptible nod.

"Have you an account of exactly which volumes were said to be on board the ship?" asked Miss Clarkson in a trembling voice.

Mary felt a moment's pity for the girl. Miss Clarkson seemed uncomfortable speaking in front of the group. She looked like a young lady given to nervous fits, and with her pale skin, brown hair, and spectacles, she was plainer even than Mary. But what did she detect behind the lenses of Miss Clarkson's spectacles? The girl's eyes glowed with an unnatural brightness that struck Mary as unhealthy.

"We cannot be certain which volumes have disappeared because we do not know precisely which ones the ship carried," replied Mr. Hartbustle gently. "Now, Mr. Spottiswoode—"

"Mr. Hartbustle!" cried Miss Clarkson with a fervor that made Mary jump in her seat. "We *need* the book! Or it will not work!" As soon as she spoke, she clasped her hands to her mouth, her eyes wide with fright.

Silence fell over the meeting as the echoes of Miss Clarkson's outburst faded.

"Miss Clarkson," said Mr. Hartbustle in a soft but steady voice, "I am very well aware of the situation." Their eyes met and Miss Clarkson nodded, hands still covering her mouth. Mr. Hartbustle turned toward Mary, a wide smile warming the entire room. "Miss Bennet, you must excuse Miss Clarkson's *enthusiasm*. The betrayal we suffered had a particularly profound effect on her. Her desire to right this great wrong sometimes overpowers her."

Mary looked at Miss Clarkson and gave the poor girl a shy smile. Miss Clarkson blinked at her, eyes growing wider.

"Now, Mr. Spottiswoode," said Mr. Hartbustle, "you had not quite finished your report, I believe?"

"Ah. Yes, yes. It is my suspicion that the ship's disappearance was caused by none other than the sorcerer now residing in Glastonbury, which means that if the volumes were onboard, he now has possession of them." He sat down with surprising grace for all of his bulk.

"Thank you, Mr. Spottiswoode," said Mrs. Post. "Mr. Callan, I believe you wished to address the group next?"

A tall, sober looking man wearing a black suit and a monocle stood up. In tones of deepest baritone he said, "I suggest we send a delegation to Glastonbury to discover the sorcerer's precise location." Mr. Callan paused and then, moving his gaze from person to person around the table, continued in a whisper, "But we must be prepared for violence should we track him down. Bravery, stealth, and strength will be our weapons, for it is our duty to the world to end this—this Glastonbury Sorcerer's *reign of terror*." He paused, allowing his words to ring through the room before continuing, "It would be my honor to lead this delegation. Who cares to accompany me?"

"I will go!" cried Lady Vinton.

"And I!" added Miss Clarkson, finally lowering her hands from her mouth.

"Very well," said Mr. Callan. "I think three sufficient for this journey. Do you agree, Mr. Hartbustle?"

"I do, Mr. Callan. This is an admirable course of action, and I suggest you depart as soon as possible. Please keep us informed of the situation by the usual method. And that, I believe, concludes the business portion of this meeting."

While the members of the Coven gathered around the small table at the back of the room to enjoy tea and muffins, Mary caught Mr. Hartbustle's attention.

"I am afraid I must return to my sister's house," she said. "But I thank you sincerely for allowing me to attend your meeting."

"Of course, Miss Bennet," said Mr. Hartbustle, gesturing her out of the room. "You have paid us a great compliment by joining our little gathering," he continued as he accompanied her to the shop's door. "Farewell, my dear Miss Bennet. I hope you can find more time to visit before too long."

"I will make every effort to visit again *soon*," Mary promised as she departed.

Her mind so occupied that she almost passed the small door to the magic corridor, Mary failed to notice that she was being observed from a few paces away. Once inside the dim passageway, she made her way slowly toward Bond Street, turning the morning's events over and over in her mind, her excitement tinged with misgivings. She could not believe the opportunity that had been granted to her—witnessing a meeting of the Bloomsbury Coven! She would never have presumed to imagine being distinguished in such a manner. Yet she lingered over memories of the coldness she had sensed from a few of the Coven's members. She wondered how such a kind man as Mr. Hartbustle could associate with such unsympathetic people. Of course, given the danger of being discovered, their coldness may simply have reflected their fear of strangers. She could not fault them for their wariness, she supposed.

Her thoughts turned next to the Glastonbury Sorcerer. He must be a villainous scoundrel to have betrayed the Bloomsbury Coven. They alluded to his treachery with such somber tones; he must have done something deplorable indeed. For the remainder of her walk she imagined the shape of his treachery, thrilling herself with her far-fetched fancies until her heart pounded. As she re-entered the bright London morning, however, she banished the increasingly horrid scenes from her mind and composed herself enough to face her family.

CHAPTER VII

On the first morning of Mary's final week in London, she was surprised by a visit from her sister Elizabeth.

"Good morning, Mary," said Elizabeth from the chamber's threshold. "May I enter?"

"Of course," Mary replied. "Please, join me by the fire." Mary laid the book she had been reading on the little table next to her, ensuring any marks identifying its contents were obscured by a deft placement. She wished to avoid questions about it from Elizabeth. But, as Mary soon discovered, Elizabeth's mission bore no relation to Mary's choice of books.

When Elizabeth had arranged herself in the chair opposite Mary, she smiled. "It has not escaped my notice," began Elizabeth, "that you have preferred to pass your time in London in solitude."

Mary blushed, feeling chagrined. Of course Elizabeth was correct. Mary had agreed to accompany the Darcys to London for her own ends. Now she saw in her sister's eyes that, as surprising as it may have seemed, her company had actually been desired.

"I did not come to chide you, my dear sister," Elizabeth continued, "but to entreat you to spare some time for me during the remainder of your visit."

"My dearest Lizzy, please forgive me. I am afraid I have been exceedingly selfish! It would give me much pleasure to honor your request."

Elizabeth favored Mary with a warm smile. "Then it is settled! After breakfast we shall pay our visits together, and the Bingleys have invited us to dine with them later. As for the rest of the week, we will provide ample entertainment for you!"

Mary proved to be so occupied during her final week in London that she found little time to pay a farewell visit to Mr. Hartbustle. For several days she accompanied Elizabeth on her round of morning visits, making an effort to be engaging without slipping into her old habit of drawing too much attention to herself. On more than one occasion, Mary caught Elizabeth looking quizzically at her as she turned down opportunities to showcase her skill on the *pianoforte*.

"I have not found time to practice in far too long to try anyone's patience with my playing," Mary confessed when Elizabeth finally questioned her. "My reading has been so engrossing. But Lizzy, it would give me great pleasure to hear you play and sing!"

"Yes, please do, Lizzy," cried Jane. "Your playing is all that is wanted to make the evening perfect!"

Mary nodded her head in vigorous agreement, happy to have Jane's support.

***

Not every evening was spent in Grosvenor Square.

The Bennet girls had received an invitation or two to dine out with families down from Hertfordshire, and Sir William and Lady Lucas insisted that Mary and Kitty accompany them to the theatre at least once before returning home. Quite happily Mary found herself sitting in a box at Covent Garden Theatre, entranced by Mrs. Siddons's Lady Macbeth. She had to stifle her giggles at the witches portrayed by men dressed as hags circling a cauldron and screeching incantations, but every time Mrs. Siddons swept across the stage, Mary was mesmerized by the actress's enchanting presence.

On her penultimate day in town, Mary found a free hour or so to slip away to the bookshop in Bloomsbury. She could not leave London without visiting Mr. Hartbustle. She wished not only to bid him a heart-felt farewell, but also to learn more about the Glastonbury Sorcerer. Mr. Hartbustle was busy helping customers, but waved to her as she entered. Seeing that he was occupied, Mary took the opportunity to wander through the shop looking at the books. She had not had the chance to peruse his shelves before, and she was impressed by what she found there: quaint books of poetry stood next to great works of philosophy, while small quartos containing plays nestled between thick works of theology. Although there seemed to be no order to the books' arrangement, Mary imagined that Mr. Hartbustle knew what each shelf contained.

"How lovely to see you again! Have you found anything that appeals to you?" Mr. Hartbustle said, opening his arms in a gesture that seemed to include the entire shop.

"I see so many books that I would love to read,"

replied Mary. "I had no idea your collection was so extensive! If only I had more time in London."

"Ah, my dear, are you to leave so soon?" said Mr. Hartbustle.

"I am afraid I must depart tomorrow."

"Then I am pleased you have chosen to spend some precious time with me! Come, let us have a bit of cake and conversation," he said, leading her to the comfortable chairs at the back of the shop and shooing the cat from his usual perch so Mary could take his place.

Mr. Hartbustle emerged from the room behind the ornate door a moment later, carrying a tray laden with a beautiful porcelain tea service, which he set on the table. "Our tea should be ready shortly," he said. "Meanwhile, your expression tells me that something is troubling you, Miss Bennet. Might I ease your mind in any way?"

Mary was taken aback. "Does my countenance reveal so much about me?" she asked.

Mr. Hartbustle nodded.

"Oh," she said, uncertain what else to say.

Mr. Hartbustle smiled at her, his eyes twinkling. "I always find," he said, "that it is best to address a topic directly."

Mary nodded. "Well then, Mr. Hartbustle, I wish to know more about the Glastonbury Sorcerer."

"Hmm. Indeed," said Mr. Hartbustle. "Which details interest you the most?"

"Who is he? And how did he betray the Coven?

"You waste no time getting to the heart of matters, do you Miss Bennet?"

Mary blushed, afraid she had overstepped the bounds of good taste.

"No, no, my child. Do not be ashamed of your inquisitive mind. It seems that too much stock is placed in false civility, whereas plain honesty no longer holds any currency." He sighed. "And yet I cannot answer your first question with complete truthfulness, for the Glastonbury Sorcerer, as you may have surmised, was once a member of our Coven. So grievous was his betrayal that we swore never to utter his name aloud. He earned his current appellation during the meeting you attended. It is, perhaps, too good a name for him, but it will serve."

Mary waited for Mr. Hartbustle to continue, but he remained silent as he poured their tea. When he had finished serving the cake, he took a sip of his tea, staring at some point in front of himself. Mary followed his gaze, but seeing nothing there, realized he must be lost in his thoughts. Gently, she repeated her question.

"How did the Glastonbury Sorcerer betray the Coven, Mr. Hartbustle?"

"I must apologize, Miss Bennet. I allowed my mind to wander," he said. But he fell silent again, appearing to weigh his words with care. Finally he sighed and said, "To understand his betrayal, you must know something of his history with the Coven." He took another sip of tea before continuing. "The Glastonbury Sorcerer came to us as a young man with grand ideas and prodigious talent. He was introduced to the Coven by Mr. Callan, whose acquaintance you made at our last meeting; they were at Oxford together. During a break in their studies, Mr. Callan invited the Glastonbury Sorcerer to visit him in London. They had discovered their shared interest in the magical arts early in their friendship, and Mr.

Callan longed to impress his new friend through his association with the Bloomsbury Coven." Again he paused to sip his tea. "The Glastonbury Sorcerer seemed the best sort of young man—intelligent, kind, and with a talent for magic that I had seen only once before. Like Mr. Callan, he was a divinity student."

Mary's raised eyebrows betrayed her surprise.

"Indeed, Miss Bennet. The Church's rumblings to the contrary, the profession has known its share of sorcerers. There is a strange kinship between theological studies and magical pursuits. After all, in both fields one must put one's faith in the unseen and the unknown. And in both fields there is a wealth of history and tradition informing each generation's practice, is there not?"

"I suppose so," replied Mary. "I have never considered the subject in such a light."

"I am sure The Glastonbury Sorcerer would agree. We were often in agreement about a wide range of topics. I must confess that I was quite taken in by him. He was a gifted sorcerer with the cleanest, most precisely executed spells you could ever hope to witness. Unlike some of the other members of the Coven, the Glastonbury Sorcerer had no interest in impressing with magical flourishes or mangling long dead languages. He proved to be a master of simplification. Yet despite certain philosophical differences, he managed to charm the entire Coven, which is, I assure you, no easy feat. Soon enough we invited him to join our ranks. Naturally he passed his trial with the greatest of ease."

"What was his trial?" Mary could not refrain from asking.

"That, my dear Miss Bennet, must remain a secret.

Only the sorcerer who has undergone the trial may reveal its details. Most choose not to."

"I see," said Mary, fighting to hide her disappointment.

"You are blameless for your curiosity, Miss Bennet, but it is not my story to tell." The old gentleman fell silent again, picking absently at the cake on his plate.

"Then what happened?" prompted Mary.

"Ah. Then followed a wonderful period of magical fellowship. Had we more time, I would enumerate the Coven's many accomplishments while the Glastonbury Sorcerer numbered among our ranks. But you have asked me a pointed question, which I endeavor now to answer. Put in the simplest terms, our fellowship ended when the Glastonbury Sorcerer encountered the power of the darkest magicks. He came to me one evening, flushed with excitement and wishing to share his discoveries. Seeing him in that agitated state of exhilaration broke my heart, for he had come to seem like a son to me. I never had any children of my own, you see. But I could ascertain at a glance that he was already lost to us. Nevertheless, I did my best to show him the danger of following that path. To my everlasting shame, I failed. He sank further and further into darkness until the Coven had no choice but to order his banishment."

Mr. Hartbustle paused, shoulders drooping. Mary thought she detected a shining in one of his eyes, as though a tear were about to spill into the teacup he cradled in his lap. Yet the old gentleman took a deep breath and continued, "I shall never forget that day, Miss Bennet. When we declared our resolution, he merely laughed at us. 'Fools!' he said. 'You know not what you do.' Then he swept out of our little meeting room. We thought, naively I know now, that we would never hear from him again, that his parting words had been sheer bluster. But that very night he found his way back into my shop and stole an ancient book that I had inherited from my grandfather. The book was the only existing copy of an important magical text, and I believe that he has made use of it since to anticipate our every action.

"I am at fault, Miss Bennet. I should have recognized him for what he is—intelligent and talented, yes, but also ravenous for power, and therefore posing the utmost danger to any sorcerers practicing magic for the greater good." Mr. Hartbustle turned his gaze on Mary, who saw the faintest hint of fever in it. "I struggle to forgive myself for allowing such a beast to be unleashed on the world. Had it not been for my tutelage, perhaps he would have remained content with his theology and minor magic. But I pushed him to the edges of his ability. You must understand how important it is that I recover the book he stole and that I make amends for the great wrong I have done."

Mary's heart broke for Mr. Hartbustle. In his anguish, his ordinarily animated spirits dimmed. Instead the man who sat before her appeared spent and broken.

"Mr. Hartbustle," she said, "you must not deride yourself so. I cannot believe that you had any part in his turn toward darkness. No man may blame another for the consequences of his own actions."

Mr. Hartbustle sighed. "My dear, you are wise beyond your young years. Of course what you say is correct, and I thank you for giving me such kind and sensible counsel."

A thrill passed through Mary. No one had ever called her wise or thanked her for her counsel. She turned a grateful eye on Mr. Hartbustle.

"And I must thank you, Mr. Hartbustle, for sharing this story with me. You may trust that I will not betray your confidence. And if *I* may, I should like to be of service to you and the Coven."

"A generous offer indeed, Miss Bennet!" cried Mr. Hartbustle. "I am certain that a time will come when I shall ask you to fulfill it. But for now, I require only the pleasure of your company."

They sat in silence for several moments, lost in thought. Mary endeavored to understand the feelings coursing through her. Her compassion for Mr. Hartbustle was coupled with anger toward the sorcerer who had caused this sweet old bookseller so much pain. She made a silent vow to contribute in whatever small way she could to Mr. Hartbustle's cause.

"Goodness!" she cried as she glanced at the clock sitting on a shelf nearby. "I am afraid I must return to my sister's house before anyone begins to wonder at my absence."

"Of course," said Mr. Hartbustle, rising to accompany her out.

When they reached the door to his shop, Mary turned an earnest face toward him. "I shall miss you, Mr. Hartbustle. May I write to you?"

"Of course you may! Do not fret, my dear," he continued as though sensing Mary's thoughts. "You need not feel alone in your studies. Through our correspondence I shall offer whatever advice I may. And from time to time should I find myself near

Hertfordshire, traveling in search of rare texts for a few of my customers, perhaps we may use such an occasion to meet."

"That would please me excessively, Mr. Hartbustle," replied Mary, beaming.

"And now, my dear, though you must be off, I beg that you wait one moment more." He hurried to the counter and ducked behind it. When he returned to her side, he carried a small book. "I cannot tell you what a pleasure it is to have made your acquaintance, Miss Bennet. Please accept this trifle as a token of our friendship." He handed Mary the book. "I await our correspondence with great anticipation!"

"Thank you, Mr. Hartbustle! A thousand times thank you! I shall write as soon as I may!" said Mary, shaking the gentleman's proffered hand, while cradling the book with the other.

He gave her a small bow as he opened the door to the shop. "Safe travels, my dear Miss Bennet. Until we meet once more!"

Still in a daze of thoughts, she made her way back through the corridor of doors to Grosvenor Square. When she arrived at the door marked "Bond Street," she lingered a moment, relishing her final moments in the shadowy passage. Then with a sigh, she opened the door and returned to the busy London streets. As she turned into Grosvenor Square, she saw a young man leaving Mr. Darcy's townhouse, his path certain to intersect hers. She gasped when she realized that he was the same young man from the ball and the street outside Mr. Hartbustle's shop. Determined to discover his identity, she marched forward. But the young man slipped away. He had been following a rather portly gentleman, and Mary lost sight of him. When the way cleared, the young man was nowhere to be found.

"So curious!" she said to herself. "I must ask Lizzy about him. Surely he is known to her." She increased her pace and arrived at Mr. Darcy's house a moment later.

"Mary Bennet!" cried Mrs. Bennet upon Mary's arrival in the parlor. "Where on earth have you been?"

"Strolling in the park, Mama. And reading," replied Mary.

"So you have said before, Mary Bennet. Whatever is so fascinating about that park?"

"There are several excellent hidden places to enjoy a book, Mama," said Elizabeth. Turning to Mary she added, "You seem in want of a cup of tea, Mary. Perhaps you will join us this afternoon?"

"I believe that is exactly what I should like," said Mary, grateful for her sister's aid.

As Mary found a seat and accepted a cup of tea, Mrs. Bennet resumed her conversation. "As I was saying," she began, "had we only the chance to become acquainted with Mr. Huntley, I should have felt comfortable inviting him to dinner before your father pays him a visit in the vicarage."

"Who is Mr. Huntley?" asked Mary.

"He is a friend to Mr. Darcy from their days at Oxford and the new vicar of our parish," replied Mrs. Bennet. "Did you not pass him on the street? Apparently he parted only moments before you arrived."

"I cannot know if I passed him or not as I have never seen him before," replied Mary, struggling to keep her countenance blank.

"Oh, Mary, always so practical," came her mother's response. Mrs. Bennet sighed and then began attacking the topic anew, her indignation growing with every word.

Mary affected listening, but heard nothing of the conversation. Instead her mind raced with the events of the day. She had not had time to comprehend the importance of everything she had learned from Mr. Hartbustle about the Glastonbury Sorcerer. Now she was faced with this new information that the mysterious young man would be settling in Hertfordshire. Some instinct she did not understand had prompted her to remain silent regarding her brief interaction with him, although the knowledge that he was to be the new vicar was startling. What would it mean to the parish that the new vicar had at least a passing familiarity with magic? What might it mean to Mary to have a fellow sorcerer in her neighborhood? She wished nothing so much as to retreat to her room and turn the events over in her mind, undisturbed by her mother's voice. But Mary sighed, knowing that she would not be excused until it was time to dress for dinner. Sipping her tea, she pretended to listen to her mother speak.

When she was finally released from the interminable afternoon in the parlor, Mary, who never required much time to dress, retired to her room and sat by the fire, glancing through the book Mr. Hartbustle had given her. It was titled simply *Magick* and seemed very old, containing ancient lore and a few difficult spells. She looked forward to exploring it once she had returned to the quiet of Hertfordshire. She had experienced enough of London's pleasures and longed for the solitary study that marked her days at Longbourn. She would miss Mr. Hartbustle, but she hoped that their correspondence would be a lengthy and frequent one. Meanwhile, she decided that for the final evening of her visit, she must turn her complete attention to her family. With that intention, she went down to dinner determined to meet everyone with a cordial face.

CHAPTER VIII

The journey home passed without excitement. Mary gazed out the carriage window, seeing little of the countryside as it flew past. Since leaving Hertfordshire she had made considerable progress in her magical studies, and with the books she had acquired in London tucked safely into her luggage, she anticipated advancing further at home. More pressing was her desire to meet the new vicar and to ascertain for herself whether he could be an ally in magic. She knew that he had recognized the spells she performed at the ball, but whether or not he was himself a sorcerer, she had yet to discover. Afraid to betray too keen an interest, she had not enquired about him, although she had been tempted to raise the topic at dinner the night before. But her mother had provided conversation enough on the subject, and Mary had learned that Mr. Huntley had taken his divinity degree from Oxford where he had been well respected by his peers. Mr. Darcy had nodded his agreement, saying nothing further as though not wishing Mrs. Bennet to continue on the subject. Nevertheless, Mrs. Bennet *had* continued by repeating knowledge already shared by her family: that Mr. Huntley had a fortune of his own and that his mother was niece to a baronet. No mention of his magical abilities had been made by anyone. Of course Mary knew that if he were a sorcerer, he would not have shared that information even with as intimate a friend as Mr. Darcy seemed to be.

On the drive back to Hertfordshire, Mary wondered again how to satisfy her desire for a magical fellowship like that shared by the members of the Bloomsbury Coven. Her fancy had led her to hope for an invitation to join the esteemed group, but when she pictured them gathered in the little room at the back of Mr. Hartbustle's shop, a shiver had run up her spine. Aside from Mr. Hartbustle, she had found the Bloomsbury Coven's members unwelcoming and not a little frightening. With a sigh, she acknowledged that she had been relieved by the imaginary invitation's failure to appear. Mr. Hartbustle's promise of a correspondence had been enough to gratify her.

"Well, Mary, you are nearly home," said Elizabeth, startling Mary from her reverie. With a kind smile she continued, "I hope that your stay in London afforded you as much pleasure as it did me. Perhaps we can persuade you to favor us with a visit to Pemberley? Kitty will be there, and Jane is always nearby."

"My goodness, Lizzy," cried Mrs. Bennet. "You have certainly taken an interest in Mary! I suppose she may be spared to visit you next year, should her situation allow it, but for now we have need of her here."

"Indeed, Mama?" said Mary. "What occasion can

be so urgent that it requires my immediate presence?"

"You shall see in good time, Mary," said Mrs. Bennet patting her daughter on the knee.

Mary looked at Elizabeth, who smiled and said, "I believe she has begun scheming to find you a husband, Mary."

"I have done no such thing, Elizabeth!" exclaimed Mrs. Bennet. "I merely wish for Mary's company in the evenings now that Kitty will return to your care. May a mother not desire to spend time with her child?"

Mary and Elizabeth exchanged arch looks, but said nothing.

At last Longbourn itself appeared, rising in the distance, the sun glinting off its windows. Before Mary knew it, she was being ushered inside her beloved home. Had she been a more sentimental young woman, she might have wandered through the house drawing her hand along a familiar banister or inhaling deeply and declaring herself adamantly opposed ever to leaving these environs again. Instead, Mary merely smiled and followed her mother to the drawing room where their father awaited their arrival.

"My family returns," he declared. "Well, have you left London aching from your absence?"

"Mr. Bennet, I shall attribute the levity in your tone to your happiness at our homecoming," said Mrs. Bennet. "Now, girls, I expect you would like to refresh yourselves before tea."

As Mary turned to leave, Mr. Bennet caught her attention. "A package arrived for you this morning, Mary," he said. "I believe it is in your room. From its shape and size, I have discerned that it is a book."

"Thank you, Papa," said Mary, and betraying none

of the excitement she felt, she walked calmly from the room. Once out of the family's sight, however, she raced up the stairs and down the hallway to her room. The package sat on her small dressing table. She hurried to open it, expecting to find a note from Mr. Hartbustle. But her expectation went unfulfilled. When she saw the title, *The Mysteries of India*, she gasped. Could this be one of the texts stolen by the Glastonbury Sorcerer?

Caution tempered her exhilaration and Mary rushed to lock her door. Clutching the book, she sat at her desk and carefully opened it. From the title page she learned that she held another of Mr. A. H.'s works. On the following page she found a dedication: *To the Honorable Nishant Rangarajan: with profound gratitude across the centuries.* She lingered over the unusual name. Surely Mr. Rangarajan was not English. But before she had a chance to delve any deeper into the book, a knock sounded at her chamber door.

"Miss Mary?" came Sarah's voice. "Your mother requests your presence downstairs."

"Thank you, Sarah," Mary called through the door. "I shall attend her presently." She listened for the sound of Sarah's footsteps retreating down the hallway. When she was certain the maid had disappeared, Mary hid the new book in her wardrobe, unlocked her door, and left her room.

Tea was being laid when Mary entered the drawing room.

"Well, Mary, are you not going to tell us?" asked Mrs. Bennet upon Mary's entrance. "What was in the package?"

"A book," Mary replied, taking her customary seat by the window.

"Gracious, Mary," said Mrs. Bennet, "I simply do not understand your passion for books."

"Naturally, my dear," intoned Mr. Bennet from his chair by the fire, "one who never reads cannot understand the pleasure another takes in the written word." He winked at Mary and returned to his book.

Mrs. Bennet affected not to hear him. Smiling, Elizabeth and Kitty turned away from their mother, and Mary grinned at her father.

The afternoon passed in pleasant conversation, and Mary discovered how much she would feel the loss of her sisters. With them gone, Mrs. Bennet was almost certain to turn all of her attention toward her remaining daughter. Remembering what her mother had said in the carriage, Mary looked forward to the following weeks with a small measure of dread, softened only by the excitement prompted by the mysterious book's arrival.

Although Mary longed to return to her room after dinner to retrieve her book, she resisted, afraid that her face might betray too much and inspire unwanted observation from her family. Instead, she sat at the *pianoforte* for the first time in months. Her fingers felt clumsy as she began playing, but she did not mind. Soon enough she lost herself in the music, letting her fingers find their way around the keys.

"Goodness, Mary!" cried Elizabeth, startling Mary. "You claimed not to have practiced in months, but you play better than ever before! So much life and feeling in your playing."

"Indeed," said Mr. Bennet. "I thought Lizzy had decided to play for us, but when I looked up I saw you there, Mary."

Mary blushed. "Perhaps one may practice too

much," she said, "and a little time away from the instrument is necessary."

"Please continue, Mary," said Elizabeth.

Delighted, Mary resumed her playing, Elizabeth joining her at the instrument.

The evening passed in relative comfort, but eventually the time came to retire. Mary bid her family a fond good night and retreated to her chamber, reflecting on the similarity between this evening and the fateful one several months before when she discovered the first book still hidden in her wardrobe. Again she waited in her room for signs that the other members of her family were tucked safely in their beds before lighting a candle and freeing the new book from its hiding place.

Beyond ascertaining the sender's identity, her first concern was determining whether or not this was one of the texts sought by the Bloomsbury Coven. A cursory glance at the table of contents revealed that it contained no spells or other magical instruction. Instead it seemed to describe the history of magic in India, leading Mary to conclude that it most likely was not. But wishing to be certain, she resolved to withhold her final judgment until she had read the book.

Several pages in, Mary learned the identity of the book's sender when she found a short note addressed to her.

Dear Miss Bennet,

I urge you to take any actions in your power to ensure the safety of this volume. Above all, let no one know that you have received it. Not everyone you meet deserves your trust.

Yours sincerely,

A. H.

Unfortunately, the note raised more questions than it answered. Why had the book's author sent her the book with this entreaty to keep it safe? How had he learned her identity? What did he mean by *not everyone deserves her trust*? Who *was* this mysterious Mr. A. H.? As the questions tumbled through her mind, Mary realized that her life had taken the sort of adventurous turn she had read about in novels. Yet she knew her heart pounded more from fear than delight. To still her mind's racing and her heart's fluttering, Mary closed her eyes and took a deep breath. When she opened them, she turned her gaze upon her candle, returning to the stillness she had learned through practicing magical meditation. After a few moments had passed, she felt herself growing calmer and resumed reading.

Her pulse quickened again as she reached the end of the book's introduction:

> *No chronicle purporting to examine the history of magic in India can be deemed complete without touching upon the subject of Indian Blood Magic. As I hope to demonstrate, most Indian mages and sorcerers dedicate their magic to healing and to serving all forms of life. However, there exist some unfortunate exceptions to that rule. Several Indian covens employ a form of magic so barbaric and violent that it requires blood sacrifices in the*

> *performance. This is magic at its most dangerous, and therefore most thrilling, which appeals to certain types of sorcerers. But readers, be warned: few manage to come away from such a practice unmarked.*

Shivering at the fearful words she had just read, Mary drew a blanket around her shoulders. Perhaps her initial assessment had been faulty and this *was* a work she should immediately send to Mr. Hartbustle and the Bloomsbury Coven. She dreaded what might happen if the Glastonbury Sorcerer ever learned of Indian Blood Magic's existence.

That thought sent Mary out of her bed and to her writing desk. She pulled out a sheet of paper and checked the point of her favorite quill pen. Her hand was poised above the inkpot when she remembered the unnatural shining of Miss Clarkson's eyes at the mention of the missing books. The memory unsettled Mary enough to stay her hand and put away her writing implements. She decided to investigate further before troubling Mr. Hartbustle about the book's arrival.

After climbing back into bed, she turned to the chapter entitled *Indian Blood Magic*. Balancing intrigue with horror, she read on.

> *For centuries sorcerers around the world have debated the merits of Indian Blood Magic. As its name suggests, sorcerers employ blood to fuel their magic. In its purest form, Indian Blood Magic can be used for truly beneficial ends. It includes several potent healing spells that can save even the most*

critically ill. The best doctors often have at least a passing knowledge of this form of magic.

The controversy surrounding Indian Blood Magic arises from its darker uses in which the sorcerer employs fresh blood gathered from a newly sacrificed victim to perform his spells. In all but the darkest of spells, an animal's blood will serve the sorcerer's wicked purposes. However, the most dreadful magic calls for blood taken from a human being, especially that of a virgin or an infant. The blood, once gathered, may be applied in a number of ways. Some spells allow the sorcerer to control the actions of others through trances. With blood taken from their victims, sorcerers can also inflict great pain across large distances without the use of a poppet to anchor the spell. The most powerful curses, such as those causing instant death, depend for their power on blood taken from an infant. The sheer horror involved in procuring such blood feeds the magic, rendering it overpowering.

The definitive text on Indian Blood Magic, "Blood Magicks," was written by the great thirteenth century Indian mage Nishant Rangarajan. Regrettably, this rare book, with only one or two copies thought still in existence, seems to have disappeared, perhaps forever.

Mary closed the book and, realizing she had been holding her breath, let out a sigh. She had never considered that such malice could exist in the world. A moment's terrible sadness threatened to overpower her. How could anyone think to use magic for such hideous ends and in such a terrifying manner?

As she blew out the candle, she knew that her sleep, should it ever come, would be plagued by horrible visions.

CHAPTER IX

*S*tanding next to her mother, Mary heard Mrs. Bennet sigh as the carriage drove away the next morning, bearing two of her daughters and her son-in-law north to Derbyshire. The leave-taking had been warm; even Mr. Darcy expressed his regret that their visit must end. But Pemberley awaited them, and at last Elizabeth, Kitty, and Mr. Darcy had climbed into the carriage and begun their journey home. When the carriage had disappeared from view, Mr. Bennet guided his wife and daughter back into the house.

"I suppose it shall be very dull here indeed," Mrs. Bennet lamented when she had settled herself in the drawing room, "with everyone gone back to Pemberley, and just the three of us left at home."

"Do not fret, my dear," said Mr. Bennet. "Without a doubt you will find some entertainment. Is the new vicar not arriving soon? Surely you may expend considerable energy discussing each detail of his merits with all the ladies of the neighborhood."

Mary, whose attention had been otherwise

engaged, looked up at the mention of the new vicar. She, too, nurtured an interest in him, although she maintained her silence, not caring to be made the object of her mother's scheming.

"Indeed he is!" cried Mrs. Bennet. "Mr. Huntley should be here in less than a month's time." She cast a sly glance at Mary, who blushed. "I do hope, Mr. Bennet, that you will call on the young man so that we may invite him to dine with us soon after he arrives."

"I suppose I must," said Mr. Bennet. "For I shall never know a moment's peace until I do."

While Mrs. Bennet passed the following few weeks in an agony of anticipation, reminding her husband of his promise at regular intervals, Mary looked forward to the vicar's arrival with a mixture of curiosity and excitement. But soon enough news came that the neighborhood's population had grown by two souls. Mr. Huntley and his widowed mother had taken up residence in the vicarage, adding greatly to the general felicity of Longbourn.

"Well, my dear," proclaimed Mr. Bennet, "I believe your long vigil has ended. I am to pay a visit to the new vicar this afternoon. And once I have discharged my duty, you shall be obliged to share the news with all of the ladies. Perhaps you shall be the first to send him an invitation to take his tea with you."

"Why, Mr. Bennet, whatever should give you the notion that I care about his arrival?" replied Mrs. Bennet. "Another young man in the neighborhood, more or less, makes not the slightest difference to me."

At Mrs. Bennet's words Mary glanced across the table and met her father's eye. Smiling, she said, "But

Mama, you have spoken of nothing but the new vicar for more than a fortnight. How can you receive Papa's news with such coldness?"

"Have I?" said Mrs. Bennet. "Well, if I did make the occasional mention of him, it was only to encourage conversation. You and your father can be remarkably dull in the evening, buried in books and not making a sound beyond turning pages or clearing throats. You should not find any fault with my desire to converse rather than to sit dumbly staring at the fire."

"Indeed, my dear," said Mr. Bennet, "no one would ever accuse you of sitting in silence whatever the circumstance, but particularly when a new young man has entered the sphere of your attention."

Mrs. Bennet, in reply, excused herself, leaving Mary and her father alone. "Well, Mary," said Mr. Bennet, "shall I suppose that like your mother you are in a flurry of anticipation to greet the new vicar?"

"I should not deem my state anticipatory, Papa. However, I *do* find myself curious about the sort of man charged with guarding the well-being of our souls."

"Hmm," replied Mr. Bennet. "Indeed."

Mary regretted speaking to her father in such a manner, but, as she had no desire to reveal the source of *her* anxious excitement, she felt it best to discourage further conversation. Her father would only tease her if she pretended to share her mother's motives, and she certainly could not confide in her father that she looked forward to the arrival of a fellow sorcerer. And so she determined to maintain her silence on the subject of the new vicar until she knew better what to expect.

She did not have long to wait. The next day a breathless and agitated Mrs. Bennet appeared unexpectedly in Mary's room. It seemed that Mr. Huntley had returned Mr. Bennet's visit with astonishing alacrity.

"Please make some effort to present yourself favorably, Mary," pleaded Mrs. Bennet. "He is a handsome young man of a fair fortune and good position—his mother's uncle was a baronet! A baronet, Mary! Moreover, I am told he is a great reader, so perhaps you will find a common interest. We really may not hope for more."

Not at all thrilled by the prospect of enduring her mother's matchmaking, Mary replied, "Indeed, Mama? I am afraid I do not understand what you mean."

"Never mind," said Mrs. Bennet. "Just come along."

Mary followed her mother down the stairs, her heart racing. How should she comport herself with him? Should she pretend not to know him, or should she mention seeing him at the ball and on the street outside of Mr. Hartbustle's shop? But if she did raise the topic of the ball, how would he respond? Surely he would not discuss the spells he had witnessed—at least not in front of her parents. But if he did not, how would she assess his knowledge of the magical world? Feeling overwhelmed by the rapid succession of these questions, she stopped and drew a steadying breath.

"Mary! The vicar is waiting!" hissed Mrs. Bennet.

Struggling to compose herself, Mary followed her mother to the drawing room. The gentlemen stood as the ladies entered, and Mary's eyes went immediately to the visitor. He was a tall man of about twenty-six years with fair hair and blue eyes set in nearly perfect symmetry on either side of an aquiline nose, which, rather than marring the overall effect of his features, actually enhanced them as it was balanced by an equally strong chin. He wore a wide smile, which was both warm and inviting. When their eyes met, Mary could not help but smile in return.

"Mr. Huntley," said Mr. Bennet, "please allow me to present my wife and daughter."

Mrs. Bennet swept over to Mr. Huntley. "Mr. Huntley! We have long looked forward to welcoming you to our small neighborhood!"

"It is a pleasure at last to be here, Mrs. Bennet."

"Mary, say hello to the new vicar," said Mrs. Bennet.

"Hello, Mr. Huntley," said Mary. "I hope you are well."

"Indeed, I am quite well, Miss Bennet," said Mr. Huntley, giving her a slight bow.

Embarrassed by the blush now staining her cheeks, Mary replied with a small curtsey.

"Mr. Huntley was just telling me that he finds Hertfordshire a good deal more appealing than Somerset," said Mr. Bennet as the ladies arranged themselves in their chairs.

"Indeed?" said Mrs. Bennet. "And why is that, Mr. Huntley?"

"I find the climate much more inviting," Mr. Huntley replied. "And," he continued, "as Hertfordshire is so much closer to London, I may expect books ordered from London shops to arrive with much more haste and much less chance of being lost in transport."

Mary's blush deepened when she realized that although Mr. Huntley was speaking to her father, he was gazing at her.

"Mary, Mr. Huntley is known to be an avid reader; Mary shares that interest, Mr. Huntley," said Mrs. Bennet. She cast a significant look at Mr. Bennet and then added, "Perhaps, Mr. Bennet, you may be persuaded to exchange your seat by the fire with Mary? I am certain she would enjoy discussing books with someone as well read as you, Mr. Huntley. Would you not, Mary?"

Mary, mortified by the transparency of her mother's scheme, nevertheless took her father's abandoned chair. Mr. Huntley waited until she was seated and then resumed his chair. While in most circumstances Mary longed to discuss books with someone pronounced as devoted a reader as she, on this occasion she preferred to speak about specific events in London. However, she did not know how best to broach the subject.

With a slightly shy but thoroughly engaging smile, Mr. Huntley began, "I see we are left to our own devices, and as a conversation about books is expected of us, please, tell me, Miss Bennet, have you read anything of late that you find particularly compelling?" He cast a quick glance over at Mary's parents.

Mary, wondering at his behavior, followed his gaze. Mr. Bennet, as was his habit, sat behind his paper, unmindful of anyone else's activities. Although Mrs. Bennet seemed intent on her needlework, Mary suspected that her mother's attention was directed across the room at herself and the vicar. Her suspicions were confirmed when she saw her mother cast a surreptitious glance in their direction. When Mrs. Bennet met Mary's eyes, she hastily bent back over her work. Sighing, Mary turned back to Mr. Huntley. Talk of the ball would have to wait.

"I have, indeed. I have a wide range of interests," she replied, not wishing to reveal too much in front of her mother. "And you, Mr. Huntley?" She was surprised by the ease she felt in conversing with him.

"I tend to read widely in the area of history. Of late I find the history of *India* to be especially intriguing." Again Mr. Huntley looked toward Mrs. Bennet and then turned back to Mary. "India guards many secrets, Miss Bennet. The entire continent exudes mystery."

Mary's eyes widened. Was this merely polite conversation, or was Mr. Huntley attempting a more significant communication? She decided she must tread carefully. Maintaining a steady voice, she replied, "Indeed? It is a topic of which I have *almost* no understanding. Have you any particular reason for your interest?"

Mr. Huntley nodded. "As a child I traveled widely with my parents. My father served as vicar for a community of English merchants in India. While we lived there, he made frequent journeys to some of the continent's more remote locations and ministered to the people of the villages. I often had the privilege of accompanying him."

"Fascinating, Mr. Huntley!" cried Mary.

"Yes, Miss Bennet. You may certainly use such a term to describe my experiences. Even as a young boy, I knew I witnessed mysteries beyond our English comprehension. Shortly before we were to return to England, my father befriended a holy man in a small village. We might term him a sorcerer, but to his people he was sacred. They saw nothing to fear in what he did. Nor did I, Miss Bennet."

Something in his tone sent a shiver of understanding through Mary. Although she knew she sat before the fire in her family's comfortable house, for just a moment, her world slid away, and Mary found herself gazing around a foreign village surrounded by a dense jungle. The sensation passed just as quickly as it arrived, and Mary, heart pounding, grasped the arms of her chair.

"Are you well, Miss Bennet?" Mr. Huntley whispered, concern coloring his voice.

"Yes, yes, I am fine," she answered. "I was just a bit faint for a moment. Perhaps it is the heat from the fire."

"Indeed, perhaps. The day is fine and warm for the season," said Mr. Huntley.

Mary nodded, smiling. "I suppose, Mr. Huntley—"

But at that moment Mrs. Bennet called from across the room, "Mary, Mr. Huntley, tea has been served!"

Mary looked at Mr. Huntley, whose face betrayed nothing although his eyes met hers. "I hope we may continue this conversation again. It seems we have much more to discuss."

"I should like that very much."

"So, Mr. Huntley," said Mrs. Bennet when everyone had been given tea, "it seems you and Mary had topics enough to discuss. I am not much of a reader myself, but Mary and her older sister Elizabeth seem to have inherited the tendency from Mr. Bennet."

"So it seems," replied Mr. Huntley.

"Were there many avid readers among the congregation in Glastonbury?" asked Mrs. Bennet.

"I suppose so. Everywhere I have been, I believe the young ladies profess to read widely."

"Profess, indeed," said Mr. Bennet. "Anyone may *profess* to read widely."

Mr. Huntley smiled but remained silent while Mrs. Bennet laughed. "Oh Mr. Bennet, the ideas you have!"

Mary spent the rest of Mr. Huntley's visit searching for an opportunity to resume their conversation. But her efforts proved fruitless. Soon after tea, Mr. Huntley excused himself. "I must return to the vicarage, I am afraid. I have household matters to settle and a sermon to compose."

"We look forward to the service this Sunday, Mr. Huntley," said Mrs. Bennet.

"I thank you, Mrs. Bennet, Mr. Bennet. Miss Bennet," he said, turning to Mary, "I hope we find another occasion to resume our discussion." And, tipping his hat, he left.

"Oh my, Mary!" exclaimed Mrs. Bennet, clapping her hands. "Such a handsome man, and he appears to be quite taken with you! I shall not question it, for it is strange indeed, but perhaps the incessant reading of sermons has finally worked to your advantage!"

Mary, who sat lost in her thoughts, merely nodded at her mother, having not heard a word she said.

"Goodness, Mary! You do not appear at all excited by his attentions!"

"My dear, leave the girl alone. I do not believe her imagination carries her from friendly conversation to holy matrimony with quite the alacrity of yours."

Mrs. Bennet shook her head. "If you are not

concerned about the fate of your daughter, Mr. Bennet, I do not know what we shall do! Remember the entail!" With her final, ominous warning, Mrs. Bennet stormed from the room.

Mary looked at her father. "I am sorry, Papa."

"Do not apologize for your mother's folly, child," came her father's reply. He gave her a searching look. "Mary—"

His question was interrupted when Mrs. Bennet rushed back into the room. "Mr. Huntley left his card. His given name is Alfred. Mr. Alfred Huntley. Not an unattractive name at all, I should say," proclaimed Mrs. Bennet. "It may serve."

Mary took the card, which read *Mr. Alfred Huntley, Vicar*. She gasped. Mr. A. H. Could he be the same Mr. A. H., author of texts magical and historical? Was she then correct in thinking their conversation had been filled with significance? He must be the one who had sent her those books, Mary thought, for he had clearly recognized her activities at the ball, and she had learned them from *his* book. Her heart leapt as she realized that with him so close she could consult him with all of her questions, and surely he could help her find a way to use her magical talents for worthy pursuits. His arrival from Glastonbury seemed perfectly timed.

Glastonbury! Mary froze as the next thought took shape in her mind: could the kind young vicar, the man she believed was the mysterious Mr. A. H., *also* be the Glastonbury Sorcerer? The vicar seemed to know a great deal about India, and according to the Bloomsbury Coven, the Glastonbury Sorcerer had stolen some important Indian books about magic. She trembled, remembering the hushed tones and frightened awe with which the members of the Bloomsbury Coven had spoken of their enemy. That meeting had taught her to be frightened of him. Yet Mr. Huntley appeared to be such a gentle man, and when she first saw him at the ball, he had seemed so disappointed in her for using magic to amuse herself at the expense of others. Of course, Mary thought, one cannot always judge by outward appearances; after all, everyone had thought Mr. Darcy scorned Lizzy when he had loved her quite deeply.

And then there were the two books that she had received, both written by him, at least one of them sent to her by his hand. Why would he have done so? With these questions to ponder, Mary spent the evening deep in thought, pretending to read as her mother rehearsed everything she believed about the new vicar. Only pieces of Mrs. Bennet's musings reached Mary: "Handsome! Soon settled, I am sure. All my daughters well married!"

Finally Mary arrived at an answer so simple she could not believe she had overlooked it: she would write to Mr. Hartbustle! He would know immediately if the Glastonbury Sorcerer had taken up residence in the vicarage of Longbourn.

"I believe I shall retire for the evening," she announced.

"So early?" cried Mrs. Bennet.

"The evening has advanced perhaps more than you imagined, my dear," said Mr. Bennet. "Good night, Mary."

"Good night, Papa, Mama."

A few moments later Mary sat at her writing desk with her pen poised once again to compose a letter to Mr. Hartbustle. She felt a thrill pass through her as she imagined the dangers arising from the Glastonbury Sorcerer's presence in Hertfordshire. She found the sensation far from unpleasant. Here was an adventure that would disrupt the monotony of her country life! And then Mary's thoughts turned to Mr. Huntley's kind blue eyes and warm smile. A familiar sensation fluttered through her mid-section, a sensation first prompted by an act of kindness by her sister's husband, Mr. Wickham.

Mary returned pen and paper to their homes, again postponing her correspondence with Mr. Hartbustle. Unwilling, or perhaps unable, to acknowledge the true reason for her actions, she convinced herself that she could be more useful to the Bloomsbury Coven if she learned more about Mr. Huntley. She would write to Mr. Hartbustle only when she could supply her friend with the knowledge he needed to capture the Glastonbury Sorcerer.

CHAPTER X

Although the following weeks provided Mary with many opportunities to observe Mr. Huntley, she failed to gather any information that might aid the Bloomsbury Coven. After his first visit to Longbourn, Mr. Huntley had been so occupied with the business of settling in a new parish that he had had little time to spare for tea with the Bennet family, so Mary had to content herself with watching him in his pulpit where his conduct reflected perfectly his role in the neighborhood. She felt the loss of his company more keenly than she cared to admit—not solely because it robbed her of the chance to determine the truth about his identity. At the very least, she remained impatient for an explanation of the events in London.

Mary knew her most pressing question could be answered with a simple letter to Mr. Hartbustle. He could tell her immediately if Mr. Huntley was the Glastonbury Sorcerer, and on more than one occasion guilt drove her to her writing desk. But each time she reasoned her way out of composing the letter she knew she should write.

Mrs. Bennet, meanwhile, insisted that they attend church far more frequently than had been their habit. From the family's pew Mary had a clear view of the vicar as he led the small congregation in their devotion. Many were the times her cheeks burned as she felt Mr. Huntley's eyes resting on her. His attention did not go unnoticed by Mary's mother.

"Mary, Mr. Huntley seems charmed by you! I believe his eyes never left you this morning," proclaimed Mrs. Bennet at dinner one afternoon.

Blushing, Mary replied, "You must be mistaken, Mama. I did not notice the vicar paying me any more attention than anyone else."

"Goodness, Mary! How could you not notice! Mrs. Long mentioned something of the sort to me the other day. 'My dear Mrs. Bennet,' said she, 'I believe you may soon be preparing for another wedding!'"

Mr. Bennet chuckled. "I cannot believe that Mrs. Long would say anything of the sort to you, my dear, even if she saw the vicar proposing to Mary on one knee."

"Mr. Bennet, I shall thank you for keeping your opinion to yourself," said Mrs. Bennet. "Now, Mary," she continued, turning back to her daughter, "we have been invited to the vicarage for dinner in a few days. I advise that you wear your green dress. It shows you off to your best advantage."

"Of course, Mama," Mary replied, her calm voice hiding the exhilaration coursing through her. Finally the opportunity she had long awaited! Finally she could be of use to Mr. Hartbustle and the Bloomsbury Coven! If she had examined her feelings further, she might have discovered they had a far different source.

"And what should I wear, my dear?" said Mr. Bennet, smiling at Mary.

"It makes little difference to me," said Mrs. Bennet. "I had not thought you would come."

"I was invited, was I not?"

"Yes, Mr. Bennet. You have been invited. But you rarely accept such invitations. I thought you would prefer a solitary evening at home."

"I do not know what could have given you that idea," said Mr. Bennet. "I enjoy the vicar's company. He has far more sense than any other young man in the neighborhood. So it is settled. I will join you."

Mrs. Bennet sighed and sipped her tea. Mary caught Mr. Bennet's eye and smiled.

"I am glad you will join us, Papa," she said. "It seems the house may be very quiet in our absence."

"Yes, Mary, I suppose it will be. But I must do my paternal duty and escort you and your mother to the vicarage. I look forward to an amusing evening."

Mary anticipated more than mere amusement and spent the following two days counting the hours until the promised dinner. She wondered what sort of woman she would find in Mrs. Huntley. She had seen the vicar's mother at the church, but always from a distance. Mrs. Huntley was no longer a young woman, but even from across the church, Mary sensed strength in her movements. She could not be sure, but Mary thought she saw a twinkle in Mrs. Huntley's eyes that reminded her of Mr. Hartbustle. Did Mrs. Huntley know about her son's magic? Did she know that her son might be the Glastonbury Sorcerer? Mary was impatient to learn more.

The day of the dinner finally arrived, and Mary dressed with care, allowing her mother's maid to help fashion her hair. She looked at herself in the mirror and smiled. She had found a spell for improving her eyesight and no longer required her spectacles. No one in the family seemed to have noticed.

"Come along, Mary!" said Mrs. Bennet when Mary arrived downstairs. "We do not want to be late!"

"Where is Papa?" asked Mary.

"He has changed his mind and prefers to dine at home." Mrs. Bennet sounded pleased. Mary assumed Mrs. Bennet was happy to be free from Mr. Bennet's disapproving eye, and she believed her mother had expended much effort in convincing her father to stay at home.

Although the vicarage was not far from their house, Mrs. Bennet insisted upon taking the carriage "to remind the vicar and his mother of *our* worth."

They were greeted by Mrs. Huntley, who ushered them inside with perfect civility. "Welcome," said Mrs. Huntley. "Please do come in. I must apologize for my son's absence. One of his parishioners fell ill, and the family has sent for Alfred. I look for his return at any moment."

"Such a pleasure at last to make your acquaintance," cried Mrs. Bennet. "And I must apologize for Mr. Bennet's absence. Some pressing business regarding Longbourn has detained him."

"Indeed? Well, we shall have to find another occasion to deepen our friendship with Mr. Bennet. My son and I enjoyed his last visit."

Mrs. Bennet beamed in answer.

"But we must not remain here in the draft! We shall wait for Alfred in the parlor," said Mrs. Huntley, leading the Bennet ladies down an ample hallway.

When they arrived at their destination, Mrs. Huntley drew Mary aside and whispered, "I am especially pleased to meet you, Miss Bennet."

Mary reacted to these words by blushing. "And I you," she managed to say, hoping her blush was not visible in the dimness of the corridor.

Mrs. Huntley smiled, squeezed Mary's hand, and then invited her into a room made cozy by the golden glow of lamps lit against the growing gloom of the late afternoon. A fire burned brightly in the hearth, casting its warmth into the room's corners. The room was furnished with comfortable chairs, a bright rug, and several small tables. Books of all shapes and sizes decorated the parlor including a number of thick volumes stacked next to a large chair that Mary guessed was the vicar's favorite. Craning her neck for a better view, she could see the title of only the top book, written in an elaborate hand with golden letters: *God's Houses in England: a Comprehensive Study of the Churches and Chapels of the Glorious British Isles by Albert Huntley*. Mary supposed the author to be Mr. Huntley's father.

As Mary turned away from the book, a movement caught her eye, drawing her gaze back to it. Was it her imagination, or had the title just wavered as though the air surrounding the book was hotter than that of the rest of the room? Examining the book Mary saw another set of words moving underneath the title, clearly vying for position. As she continued to stare at the book, the other title swam to the forefront just long enough to allow her to read it: *Blood Magicks by Nishant Rangarajan, translated by Oliver Dudley*. Then the first title seeped back into place, and the wavering dissipated. Mary, her breath suspended and eyes wide, stood very still. If her eyes had not deceived her, Mary had just discovered a lost book of darkest magic hidden by the Palimpsest Spell. She had read about this spell for hiding books within other books in *Magick*, the book given to her by Mr. Hartbustle before she left London. Unlike the simple glamour she used to hide the titles of her books, this spell required skills she longed to master. For a moment her excitement obscured the reason for her presence in the vicarage, and Mary thought only of what this sorcerer might teach her.

But the excitement soon became amazement, as Mary wondered how anyone could have cast that spell. Only passing references to its existence remained in books—according to *Magick*, the Palimpsest Spell had faded into legend. Perhaps Mr. Huntley had not the slightest inkling that he had an active Palimpsest Spell in his library. Yet if he did possess knowledge of it—if he had indeed cast that spell—she would have proof that, at the very least, a powerful sorcerer now lived nearby. His custody of the book itself almost confirmed Mary's more dreadful suspicions about the vicar's true identity.

She peered again at the book, hoping to see its proper title once more, but she was disappointed. As she stepped forward, desiring to a closer view, she felt a chill run up her spine. Looking back, she saw Mrs. Huntley watching her, a small smile playing on the older woman's lips.

"You have noticed my son's weakness, I suppose," she said.

Mary's heart pounded so heavily in her chest that she felt sure everyone could hear it. She looked at

Mrs. Huntley, not believing what she had just heard.

Mrs. Huntley smiled. "He cannot finish one book without being drawn to another, and so he leaves them lying about, stacked next to chairs and strewn about his desk. The housekeeper is in a constant state of despair, but he simply tells her not to bother." She gestured for Mary to sit. "I am told that you share my son's passion for reading, Miss Bennet. I look forward to eavesdropping on your conversations about books."

Mrs. Bennet, who stood nearby, replied, "Yes, Mary is a great reader. She reads almost exclusively religious books. 'La,' I say to her, 'you will lose your eyesight and get a terrible squint if you keep reading those books,' but she reads on and on just the same. I suppose the vicar is much the same, Mrs. Huntley. Do you not despair for his eyes?"

"Ah, well, it is a mother's duty to worry, is it not, Mrs. Bennet?" said Mrs. Huntley.

"It is indeed, Mrs. Huntley," replied Mrs. Bennet. "I worry endlessly about the fate of my daughters Mary and Catherine. Their sisters have all made wonderful marriages, and Catherine, Mary's younger sister, has the good fortune to live among some of the finest families of England, so I need not fret quite so much about her prospects. But Mary prefers to stay at home, and I have begun to believe she will never leave us."

Mary blushed with mortification. Her mother, once set upon this topic, would not leave it until she had exhausted it. Now the subject of discussion, Mary gave up hope of examining the mysterious book any further. She sighed and resigned herself to an afternoon of chatter, glancing impatiently from time to time toward the chair now hiding the book from her sight.

Luckily she was not forced to endure the embarrassment long. Much to Mary's relief, her mother was interrupted by Mr. Huntley's return. Mrs. Bennet had been recounting a story concerning Mary, a *pianoforte*, and a ball at Netherfield. Mary longed to avoid the humiliation still occasioned by that particular event, so when the vicar entered the room, Mary interrupted her mother.

"Mr. Huntley, we have wondered where you were," she said.

"I beg your forgiveness. I have only just come from the bedside of Mr. Abbot. He had taken a turn for the worse, but as the day wore on, he seemed much improved. I left only a few moments ago."

He strode across the room and greeted his mother with a kiss. "I have not kept you waiting too long have I?"

"Not at all, my dear. But I believe dinner awaits us, so we must adjourn to the dining room. You may accompany Miss Bennet to the table. Her mother and I shall follow behind." Mrs. Huntley surprised Mary with a wink to Mrs. Bennet.

Mrs. Bennet's attempts at an arch nod failed. Then she raised her eyebrows at Mary, who recognized her mother's effort to communicate the moment's importance. Mary replied with a small nod. Better to keep her mother content now than to have to smooth over her anger later.

Their dinner, served by the housekeeper, Mrs. Owens, was simple and beautifully prepared. To Mary's delight Mrs. Huntley occupied Mrs. Bennet's attention, freeing her to engage Mr. Huntley in conversation.

"You have a most impressive book collection, Vicar," Mary said with outward calm while her heart raced inside her chest.

"I thank you for the compliment, Miss Bennet. My travels have afforded me the opportunity to build my collection," Mr. Huntley responded. "Are there any that interest you in particular?"

"I must confess my fondness for our English churches. I saw a beautiful book about them. If it is no trouble to you, I would very much like to borrow it," Mary replied.

"Ah, I am afraid, Miss Bennet, that of all the books in my library, I must deny you the one you most desire. It is indispensable for the research I am currently undertaking. I have other books on the subject, which I would happily place in your hands. After dinner you may peruse my library and decide for yourself. And perhaps, at a later date, I may find myself in a position to oblige your request to study the book in question."

"I look forward to the opportunity to examine it," she replied, masking her disappointment with a smile. "May I enquire about the nature of your research?" Mary surprised herself with her boldness.

"Alas, I fear I must again disappoint you, Miss Bennet. I am, unfortunately, not at liberty to discuss my work at the moment. Perhaps a time may come when I may share it with you. I beg your patience, Miss Bennet." He glanced down the table and then turned back to Mary, drawing a breath as if to speak, but he was interrupted by Mrs. Bennet.

"Mary, Mrs. Huntley has just informed me that Mr. Huntley also attended the ball the Darcys gave in your honor. You did not tell me you that you had the pleasure of meeting him before he arrived in Hertfordshire."

"That is because I did not have that pleasure, Mama. We did not meet at the ball, although I believe our paths almost crossed," said Mary.

"Indeed?" said Mrs. Huntley. "Did your paths almost cross, Alfred?"

"I seem to remember something of the sort," replied Mr. Huntley. "You were seated on the benches lining the wall, were you not Miss Bennet?"

"I was," said Mary. "I do not have a great love of dancing, so I often sit at balls."

"If I remember correctly," said Mr. Huntley, "you sat at the center of a great deal of commotion. Young men falling, ladies dropping fans, and a violinist sending his bow careening across the ballroom."

"You must be mistaken, Mr. Huntley," cried Mrs. Bennet. "My daughter's husband would never allow such commotion in his house. Surely nothing of the sort happened!"

"Indeed, Mama, the ball was quite eventful, although I would not characterize myself in Mr. Huntley's terms. Certainly, I bore witness," said Mary, "but not from the center."

"I stand corrected, Miss Bennet," said Mr. Huntley, smiling at her.

"Mrs. Bennet," said Mrs. Huntley, "do you spend a great deal of time at Pemberley?"

"Indeed, I do!" cried Mrs. Bennet whose reply was not entirely truthful, yet she was happy nevertheless to demonstrate her authority on the subject. "It is a grand house with beautiful grounds. Mr. Darcy's family has occupied it for generations. My daughter

Elizabeth now serves as its mistress."

Mary, grateful for the change in topic, remained silent for the rest of the meal, though she wondered at Mr. Huntley's purpose in addressing the events of the ball in front of her mother. She resisted the desire to communicate further and kept her eyes trained on her plate, pretending not to notice Mrs. Huntley's frequent glances in her direction. No one dared to interrupt Mrs. Bennet's enthusiastic discourse on Pemberley's wonders.

For the remainder of their visit, Mary brooded silently about the exchange at dinner and the presence of the dangerous book in the vicar's collection. Her answers to questions leveled at her by the others of the party were polite enough if somewhat brief. By the visit's conclusion, she had resolved that it was time to write to Mr. Hartbustle. She could no longer justify avoiding the task.

As soon as she arrived home, Mary went straight to her room, claiming a slight headache. After she locked her door, she sat at her desk and took out a sheet of writing paper. As she dipped her pen into the ink, she thought about how to begin. Then deciding the matter was too important for anything but the bluntest terms, she put pen to paper and wrote:

Dear Mr. Hartbustle,

I must begin this letter by apologizing for not writing to you sooner. I have suspected for some weeks now that our new vicar, Mr. Alfred Huntley, is that same Glastonbury Sorcerer so troubling your Coven. I chose to remain silent in the hopes that I might be incorrect, for I had no desire to trouble you with false alarms. But now I believe I have unassailable proof of his identity. While dining at the vicarage with my mother, I caught sight of something very disturbing. Among the vicar's collection was a book of dubious fame, hidden with the Palimpsest Spell. The book, titled Blood Magicks, may be known to you. It seems that its presence, guarded by magic of the highest order, confirms my suspicions. I humbly await your advice about how to proceed in this most pressing development.

Your friend as always,

Mary Bennet

When she finished writing, she read the letter. Satisfied with its contents, she folded it, sealed it, and addressed it to Mr. Hartbustle at his shop. Then she rang for Sarah and pressed the letter into the maid's hand with careful instructions that it should be posted as soon as possible. Sarah nodded, eyes wide, but said nothing before scurrying away. Satisfied that she had done all that she could, Mary climbed into bed where she lay awake for hours wondering what Mr. Hartbustle might advise. One thought troubled her most: she feared that he would urge her to avoid Mr. Huntley at all costs. She did not believe she could follow such advice.

CHAPTER XI

*T*o Mary's great relief, she suffered only a few days of dreadful anticipation before Mr. Hartbustle's reply arrived in the morning post. She had just risen from another fitful night when a timid knock sounded at the door.

"Yes?" Mary called.

"Miss Mary, a letter has come for you."

Mary flew to the door and opened it, taking Sarah quite by surprise and nearly sending her toppling into the room.

"Do forgive me, Sarah," Mary whispered, steadying the maid with a firm hand. "I did not mean to frighten you."

"Here it is," replied Sarah in a tiny voice, holding out the letter. "I must return to the kitchen, Miss, if it is all the same to you."

"Of course. Please make no mention of this letter, Sarah. It is terribly important that no one learns of my correspondence."

Without a word Sarah nodded and then hurried

from the room. As Mary locked her door, she experienced a brief moment of regret for making such a fuss over the letter. But it passed almost immediately. Another maid's curiosity might have been piqued into revealing Mary's secrets, but Sarah had proven herself dependable many times. Mary trusted that the girl would keep her tongue.

Mary turned her full attention to the letter clutched in her hand. In her impatience to discover its contents, she flipped it over to tear it open. But a quick glance at the seal stilled her hand. Amazed, Mary ran her fingers over the deep red wax, staring wide-eyed at the image imprinted within it. Two magnificent animals intertwined to form the letters B and C. Mary blinked, convinced her eyes had deceived her, for so life-like was their rendering that the animals seemed to move. She brought the letter to the window to study the seal under the light. It took a moment for her to realize that not one, but two giant winged lizards, possibly dragons, lay back-to-back, their tails looping around to form the curves of the letter B. What could only be a phoenix, a large bird with flames instead of tail feathers, perched on the lower portion of the B, its tail curling upward into the letter C. It was the official seal of the Bloomsbury Coven. Taking care not to mar the creatures, she gently unsealed the letter and read:

My Dear Miss Bennet,

I thank you profoundly for your most informative letter. I count myself felicitous indeed to have such a friend as you, and the Bloomsbury Coven will remain forever in your debt for this service.

I shall waste no more time in pleasantries because I must confirm your fears. The man whom you have named is indeed the same sorcerer who betrayed the Coven and stole from my shop the very book you discovered among his collection.

Miss Bennet, I fear there are no words strong enough to communicate the danger that awaits you should you stray too close to the Glastonbury Sorcerer. His outwardly pleasing form hides a soul tainted from practicing the blackest of magicks. I beg you to observe the utmost vigilance at all times, for I know how difficult avoiding the vicar of your church will prove. In your dealings with him, you must betray no knowledge of his true identity. Should he discover that you are privy to such information, he will have no choice but to eliminate you and your entire family. He cannot be trusted. I advise you, therefore, to avoid him whenever possible. However, should you find yourself in his sights, remain calm. Do nothing that could reveal what you are. He must not know that you are a member of the magical community.

Given this development, I shall journey to Hertfordshire as soon possible. Unfortunately, my business prevents my leaving immediately, but you may rest assured, Miss Bennet, that I will do everything within my power to ensure your safety and that of your family. In the meanwhile, you will find several protection charms in the books you brought home from London. I urge you to learn them as soon as possible.

I remain as ever, your friend,

H. Hartbustle

Mary folded the letter absently, her mind filled with dire images born of Mr. Hartbustle's warnings. What outrages might Mr. Huntley inflict upon her and her family? How might he punish her for her knowledge? When she remembered the events of the ball at Mr. Darcy's London house, she realized she had already defied one of Mr. Hartbustle's warnings. Should she write again and confess that it was too late, that the Glastonbury Sorcerer already knew what she was? After several moments of thought, she decided against it. She did not wish to worry Mr. Hartbustle any further.

As Mary sat staring out of her bedroom window, visions of Mr. Huntley arose in her mind one after the other. In them his gentle demeanor was replaced with an aspect of horror. His eyes, so warm and friendly, now seemed to her filled with greed and malice. How had she not seen him for what he was? How could she be so blinded by his handsome appearance and melodious voice? She sighed as tears sprung to her eyes, surprising her with their suddenness. But resolving to be strong for Mr. Hartbustle's sake and for that of the Coven, she wiped her tears away with a rough gesture and stood to dress for the day.

Before leaving her room, Mary searched through her books for the protection charms suggested by Mr. Hartbustle. She found one or two promising spells and the instructions for a charm, but she worried that they might not be potent enough should the Glastonbury Sorcerer decide to strike with his full force. She glanced at the wardrobe where she had hidden *The Magic of India*. Might she not find ideas for a better protection spell in the chapter on blood magic? She trembled, terrified by the notion. No, she could not venture in that direction. She might mean well, but she had no desire to follow Mr. Huntley's lead. *He* may be willing to compromise himself that way, but *she* was not. Sighing, she turned back to *Spells* and memorized the list of herbs necessary for the charm. After breakfast she would search for them in Longbourn's small wilderness.

When she arrived in the breakfast parlor, Mary found her mother all in a flutter.

"Mary, you shall never guess who dines with us this afternoon!"

"Indeed, Mama?" replied Mary absently.

"The vicar and his mother!" cried Mrs. Bennet triumphantly.

Mary's teacup clattered back into its saucer, spilling tea onto the table. "I am sorry," she muttered, dabbing at the tea with her napkin.

Mrs. Bennet laughed. "Goodness, Mary! You shall have to compose yourself better. And here I had begun to worry that you had no interest at all in Mr. Huntley!"

Mr. Bennet lowered his newspaper, took in the scene, and raised the paper back up without a word, but Mary thought she saw a smile spread across his face. If only they knew the truth! Yet she must protect them from it at all costs. Composing herself, she said, "The cup slipped, Mama. It was certainly not a reaction to your news. I cannot say that I am pleased by it, however. Does the vicar not have more important business than dining with us?"

"What could be more important than finding a wife?" replied Mrs. Bennet.

"My dear Mrs. Bennet," said Mr. Bennet, "the list of business more important than finding a wife would exhaust even your powers of conversation. You shall have to content yourself with your own beliefs and leave us to ours."

"Mr. Bennet, I shall never understand your mind," declared Mrs. Bennet as she rose to leave. "How can you remain calm when Mary's future happiness lies in the balance? Mary, we shall continue our conversation later." She swept from the room.

A moment passed in perfect silence. Then, without lowering his paper, Mr. Bennet said, "Fret not, my dear, your secret is safe with me."

"Papa?" said Mary, voice trembling with the effort of hiding her emotions. "Whatever do you mean? What secret?"

Mr. Bennet paused before answering. "Your affection for the vicar, Mary. It is as plain as day. But I shall not betray you to your mother. Why should we give her any more support to encourage her schemes?"

Relieved, Mary smiled. "Indeed, why should we? Thank you, Papa."

"It is my pleasure, my dear."

The rest of the meal passed with no more conversation than a request to pass the sugar, as both Mary and her father were occupied by their thoughts. Mary's mind raced as she conceived and then dismissed excuse after excuse for avoiding the dinner party her mother had arranged with so little thought given to the rest of the family's desires. Eventually, she had to admit to herself that no reason save mortal danger could release her from her obligation to sit at the table with the Glastonbury Sorcerer and his mother. So fraught were her emotions that Mary nearly giggled aloud when she reached this conclusion. For without a suitable excuse to stay in her room, she would indeed be placing herself in mortal danger.

With that thought a new set of questions arose. How many times had she longed for such excitement? How jealous had she been of the heroines of the novels she loved so well? But faced with her own adventure, she realized she simply wanted to hide. Real terror was not so thrilling, she discovered. *Real* terror was not the stuff of desire.

"Mary?"

With a start, Mary noticed that her father had lowered his paper and was addressing her.

"Are you well?" said Mr. Bennet.

"Indeed, Papa," she replied. "I must have gotten lost in my thoughts."

"As is your habit, I suppose. Perhaps you should have a rest. Your mother may never forgive you should you miss your opportunity to show yourself off to your best advantage for the vicar."

"I believe I shall take a walk, Papa. Nothing like brisk country air to cure a young lady of her woes." Mary kissed her father and left the room. A solitary ramble outside would do her some good. Besides, she had herbs to collect.

By the time Mary returned, eyes bright and cheeks red from her time out of doors, she felt steadier. While in the woodland collecting herbs, she had decided that she was not in immediate danger. Despite her anxieties she reasoned that the Glastonbury Sorcerer would do nothing to reveal his identity so soon after arriving in the village. For what other reason than to be safely tucked away from the Bloomsbury Coven could he have sought the relative anonymity of a small parish's vicarage? Those thoughts comforted her as she made her way back to the house, her dress slightly wetter than it had been when she left, her shoes somewhat muddier.

"Mary Bennet!"

Mary stopped short at the foot of the stairs. Turning, she saw her mother hurrying toward her, face red and eyes narrowed.

"Where on earth have you been? What have you been doing? You look a mess! Get upstairs this instant. I shall send Hill to attend you."

Mary had not witnessed such strong feeling in her mother since Charlotte Lucas had wed Mr. Collins. Without another word, she climbed the stairs to her room, grateful to have escaped her mother's anger unscathed.

When she was free from Hill's attentions, Mary wrapped the herbs she had gathered in her handkerchief and tied it with a ribbon, chanting quietly the words of the charm, "By the elements that be, earth and air, fire and water, I bind this charm to protect me." When the charm was complete, she slipped it into her pocket. Then she tucked herself into the window seat and began learning the simple warding spell she had found in *Spells*. By the time Sarah arrived to summon her, Mary felt confident that she could survive dinner with the Huntleys.

"I am pleased to see that you have taken this occasion seriously, Mary," said Mrs. Bennet as Mary arrived downstairs. "It is my hope that the vicar has every opportunity to observe you at your full advantage."

"I shall do my best to satisfy your hopes, Mama," said Mary.

"I believe I see them walking up the lane," came the eager reply.

Mary followed her mother's gaze out the window, her heart leaping into her throat. She slid her hand into her pocket and grasped the charm. It would have to do.

"How pleasant that you are able to join us for dinner, Mr. Huntley, Mrs. Huntley!" cried Mrs. Bennet as her guests were ushered into the drawing room. "We shall go in to dinner in a moment. Mr. Bennet had a letter to complete, but then he will join us."

"The pleasure belongs to us, Mrs. Bennet. My mother and I thank you for your generous invitation."

"Ah, here is Mr. Bennet. Mary, please show the vicar into the dining parlor."

Mr. Huntley turned to Mary, smiling. "I could not ask for a more charming guide," he said, offering his arm.

Struggling against her desire to flee, Mary took his arm. "This way, please, Vicar."

Had she imagined it or had Mr. Huntley recoiled when she touched his arm? His rapid glance down with narrowing eyes suggested that he had felt something. Could it have been the protection charm? If so, perhaps he had already attempted to harm her, but the charm had thwarted him. To keep from betraying herself, she kept her gaze focused straight ahead. "Just the next room, Vicar," she said, pitching her voice low to keep it steady.

From behind them came Mrs. Bennet's voice.

"Vicar, you shall be seated next to Mary, and Mrs. Huntley, you shall have the pleasure of Mr. Bennet's conversation."

"Then who will have the pleasure of your conversation, my dear?" asked Mr. Bennet.

"Oh, Mr. Bennet! You know how I prefer to keep silent in large parties," his wife replied.

"Indeed," came his response.

The party took their seats according to Mrs. Bennet's design. The first course was served and was sufficiently admired. As the second course was brought out, Mr. Huntley turned to Mary.

"Was your walk in the woodland this morning pleasant, Miss Bennet?"

"How did you know what I did this morning, Mr. Huntley?" asked Mary.

"My mother thought she saw you. She, too, enjoys a solitary walk."

"It was agreeable, thank you," replied Mary.

"Are there still elderberries to be found so late in the season?"

"Yes, there are," said Mary, aware of the blush now creeping up her neck. She had gathered elderberries for her charm, but how did he know? "But one needs to know exactly where to look."

"Do you like elderberries, Miss Bennet?" Mr. Huntley's voice had a chill to it.

"I prefer strawberries," Mary replied, matching his tone.

"Now Mary, you know that you love elderberries and detest strawberries," said Mrs. Bennet. "Why ever would you tell such tales to the vicar?"

"I believe that you have confused me with Lydia, Mama."

"No, I have not," insisted Mrs. Bennet.

"This mutton is so tender, Mrs. Bennet," said Mrs. Huntley. "Pray, tell me how it has been prepared."

Mary, aware that the Glastonbury Sorcerer observed her closely, heard nothing of Mrs. Bennet's reply. During the rest of the meal, she paid careful attention to the Glastonbury Sorcerer's every movement, prepared to cast a more comprehensive protection spell should the circumstances warrant it.

For his part, the Glastonbury Sorcerer ate in silence, occasionally glancing toward his mother and shaking his head almost imperceptibly. But Mary noted the anger shining in his eyes and counted the moments until dinner ended when she might be released from such close proximity to danger. Alas, that moment was not soon in coming as there were several more courses through which to sit.

But the meal finally ended and the ladies retired to the drawing room, leaving the men to their after-dinner pursuits. Mary's hand lingered on her father's shoulder as she exited the dining room. She was reluctant to leave Mr. Bennet alone with such a dangerous guest and muttered a few words of protection as she left.

"What was that, my dear?" Mr. Bennet called after her.

"I said nothing, Papa," Mary lied. "We shall see you in the drawing room soon, will we not?"

"Later, my dear. I have had few chances to speak with the vicar; I should like to take my time."

Seeing that she could remain no longer without arousing suspicions, Mary followed the other ladies to the drawing room where she glanced regularly at the door. Unfortunately, her mother noticed her glances.

"La, Mary, the vicar shall join us soon enough. Perhaps you could entertain us with a song or two at the *pianoforte*."

Happy to satisfy this wish of her mother's, Mary sat at the instrument and began playing. The music soothed her and she forgot for a little while the uncomfortable circumstances of the evening.

She had just begun playing a favorite sonata when she was aware of someone standing behind her.

"Please do not stop playing, Miss Bennet," said Mr. Huntley as Mary's fingers faltered on the keys.

Terrified by the Glastonbury Sorcerer's nearness, Mary nevertheless resumed playing, feeling his eyes on her all the while.

"May I join you, Miss Bennet?" he asked when she had finished.

"I believe I have played for long enough," Mary replied, pushing her stool back and beginning to stand, "I should not be rude and avoid conversation with your mother."

"Please, Miss Bennet. A moment longer. Am I to be robbed of the enchantment of your playing simply because I must fulfill my duty and speak to your father?" said the Glastonbury Sorcerer, hurriedly bringing a chair over to the instrument.

Mary drew on all of her strength to keep herself steady as she resumed sitting. Every instinct cried out that she should run from the room, but how would she explain such behavior to her mother? Drawing a deep breath, she placed her fingers back on the keys and began playing the first song that she could think of: a melancholy air in which she had often indulged when she was younger.

"The opportunity to discuss the ball in London

has not presented itself," said the Glastonbury Sorcerer quietly.

Mary kept her eyes fixed on the keys and did not reply.

"I do not suppose this is the place for such a discussion. We would not want your parents to overhear and realize your part in the events. But I do look forward to such a conversation soon. We have much to learn from each other, Miss Bennet," he said, his tone earnest.

Appalled, Mary stopped playing and stood suddenly. "I do not know what you mean, Mr. Huntley. I thank you for your attentions, but I am afraid I am not feeling myself this evening. If you will excuse me." Without a word to her parents or to Mrs. Huntley, Mary hurried from the room.

A few minutes after she arrived in her room, her mother stormed in. "Mary Bennet!" she cried. "What has gotten into you? Where are your manners? To run from our guests without so much as a 'by-your-leave'! To abandon the vicar, astonished, mid-conversation! What will people say?"

"I apologize, Mama. I felt a sudden illness come on, and I could not bear the heat of the room. I was afraid there might be worse consequences than rudeness affecting the vicar should I sit next to him any longer. I did not wish to embarrass you, nor did I intend to be uncivil, but I am truly ill." She ran to the basin, arriving just in time.

"Oh dear! Shall I send for the doctor, Mary?"

Mary recovered herself enough to answer. "No, thank you, Mama. I believe I shall be fine after I rest. I want nothing more than to go to my bed and sleep. Please make my apologies to our guests."

"Of course, dear. I shall send Sarah to attend you."

Wishing only to be left alone, Mary replied, "Please do not bother Sarah, Mama. I shall not need her this evening."

"If you insist. I must see what I can do to smooth over the damage. I do not know what shall become of you if you do not manage to marry Mr. Huntley!"

Mary sat in the darkening room, grateful for the peace and quiet. She let a momentary worry about her parents' welfare slip by. The Glastonbury Sorcerer had betrayed no interest in them, and Mary believed they would be safe for the duration of his visit. In the security of her room she could think about the evening's events. What had the Glastonbury Sorcerer meant by "we have much to learn from each other?" Was he attempting to draw Mary to his evil ways? If so, he would find himself sorely disappointed. She would never be swayed by dark magic, no matter how much power it promised her.

Feeling suddenly exhausted, Mary climbed into bed. Her slumber was interrupted an hour later by the arrival of a note. Mary took it into her trembling hands and dismissed Sarah. Curiosity conquering fear, she unfolded the paper and read:

Dear Miss Bennet,

I am sorry that our conversation must be postponed because of your being suddenly indisposed this evening. Rest assured that I look forward to resuming our discussion. Please do not forget what I said to you, Miss Bennet, for I believe we have much in common. It would benefit you greatly to converse with me as soon as possible.

I remain your humble servant,

Mr. Alfred Huntley

Mary shuddered as she read the note again. Why did he persist in suggesting they shared anything in common? How could speaking with him be of any benefit to her? Her mind filled with such questions, she climbed back into bed, blew out the candle, and sighed with the knowledge that she faced another restless night.

CHAPTER XII

*T*he following morning Mary sent word by Sarah that she was still too ill to join the family and that she preferred to rest undisturbed in her room. Nevertheless, she had to succumb to her mother's anxious fussing and the doctor's more rational examination before her wishes were fulfilled. Once she was finally alone, instead of returning to bed, Mary sat at her desk pouring over her books, learning every protection spell she could find. She had decided with the dawn that she could not forever shrink from the Glastonbury Sorcerer, despite Mr. Hartbustle's warnings. With the light had come courage, and she had determined that while she would not seek a confrontation, she must be prepared for one, as Mr. Huntley seemed so intent on approaching her.

That very event occurred only a few days later when Mary found herself alone in the churchyard with the Glastonbury Sorcerer. She had gone there to gather berries from the large rowan tree growing near the church. So intent on her work was she that she did not hear Mr. Huntley's approach.

"Miss Bennet?" he said.

"Oh!" she cried, startled. When she realized who had called her, Mary paled. Hastily, she fumbled in her pocket to assure herself of the protection charm's presence.

"I apologize, Miss Bennet. I had no desire to frighten you. Are you ill? You seem rather pale. Please, let me help you inside."

"I, I—" she began.

"No, do not try to speak. You look as though you might faint. Here, lean on my arm."

Trembling with a mixture of fear and excitement, Mary did as she was told and let the Glastonbury Sorcerer help her into his house.

"I am afraid my mother is not home to serve as chaperone, but as you seem so unwell, we should hardly be bound by propriety's dictates. I shall call for tea after I see you settled in a chair by the fire. You are shivering, Miss Bennet. Ah, mind your step; I am afraid the floor in my study is a little uneven in places."

Mary said nothing as he led her to a chair next to the small hearth where a fire burned heartily.

"I shall return in a moment," he said, hurrying from the room.

Mary's eyes required a moment to adjust to the darkness inside after the brightness of the day outside. When she could see clearly again, she studied her surroundings. She found herself in a small but friendly room with a large oval window in one wall that looked out onto a neatly kept garden. The other walls were lined with shelves brimming with books. Next to the chair opposite hers stood a small table laden with papers. Mary longed to examine them, but feared the Glastonbury Sorcerer's reaction should he return to discover someone rifling through his belongings. She was on the verge of dismissing that fear and investigating anyway when Mr. Huntley came striding back into the room.

"My housekeeper shall arrive in a moment with tea and cake. I hope you have warmed sufficiently."

"I have, thank you," said Mary. "I suppose this is your study?"

"It is indeed. It is the coziest room in the house, and I thought it best for warming you."

"It is a lovely room," said Mary, confused by Mr. Huntley's civility. But following his lead, she remained courteous, judging that to be the safest mode of behavior.

An awkward silence settled over them, broken only by the crackling of the fire and an occasional gust of wind causing the shrubbery to brush eerily against the walls.

"I believe the weather is turning," said Mr. Huntley. He glanced out the window. "Over there—dark clouds are sweeping in. The day had been so lovely, but now I think it will rain."

"At this time of year the weather can be unpredictable," replied Mary, astonished that she sat in the Glastonbury Sorcerer's study discussing the most English of subjects as if nothing at all were amiss.

"Miss Bennet—"

Whatever he wished to say would have to wait, as the housekeeper bustled in with a tray. Tutting under her breath, she set the tray on the desk. Then she cleared the papers from the small table and replaced them with the tea tray. Without a word she served first Mary and then her employer.

"Thank you, Mrs. Owens," said Mr. Huntley as she left. "She does not approve of my study. I look after it myself, and she believes that is improper. But I could hardly allow her the opportunity to see *all* of my work, do you not agree, Miss Bennet?"

"I—"

"You wish to tell me that you have no idea of what I speak. But you know better than that, Miss Bennet. Pray tell me, for I have been able to think of nearly nothing else since the event, what spell *did* you use to send the violinist's bow across the ballroom? It made the most impressive arc!"

Mr. Hartbustle's warning in the forefront of her mind, Mary did not immediately answer the question. While she knew better than to compromise her safety by admitting to her sorcery, she felt compelled to reply with the truth. Yet she also knew that she did not possess the strength or skill to battle the Glastonbury Sorcerer. Mary felt herself grow warm under his gaze, and more to redirect his scrutiny and end the terrible anticipation than anything else, she chose to answer honestly.

"I used your spell for moving objects, Mr. Huntley. It was the first spell I learned."

Mr. Huntley smiled. "And you performed it perfectly, Miss Bennet."

Further confused by the warmth of his praise, Mary grew impatient. "Mr. Huntley, why have you invited me here today?" she demanded.

"I should have thought that was obvious, Miss Bennet."

"And why is that?" she said.

"To begin, you seemed very unwell in the churchyard, and I wished to assist you. But more to the point, we have important matters to discuss," he said.

"No, Mr. Huntley, I am certain we do *not*." Mary knew challenging him was pure foolishness, yet she continued, "I know who you are, Mr. Huntley."

"Indeed? And who am I?" asked Mr. Huntley, eyebrows raised.

"You are the Glastonbury Sorcerer. Do not deny it, for I have proof."

Mr. Huntley stared at Mary, appearing confused, but then a smile spread across his face, and he replied, "I shall save you the trouble of elaborating on your proof. I know of what you speak, and you are not entirely incorrect. I suppose the appellation is accurate enough, as I did pass the last several years in Glastonbury, and like you, I am a sorcerer. But I am certain that you misunderstand what that means." Mr. Huntley's smile broadened.

"No, Mr. Huntley, I do not. I know that it means you practice the darkest and deadliest of magicks."

Mr. Huntley's smile vanished. "Now I understand why you muttered a protection spell when you left the dining room the other evening, but whatever could have given you the idea that I practice dark magic, Miss Bennet? That is a most serious accusation!"

Despite the fear inspired by his stern demeanor, Mary summoned her courage and continued, "I attended a meeting of the Bloomsbury Coven. There I learned of your existence and of your betrayal of them."

"I see. I suppose that explains a great deal. Certainly they would wish you to believe such a story.

It suits their ends perfectly. But I am afraid, Miss Bennet, that you have been deceived most dreadfully, especially by your friend Mr. Hartbustle. I know him of old and I know his capacity for deceit."

How did he know about her acquaintance with Mr. Hartbustle? Mary was shocked into silence, but then she remembered seeing Mr. Huntley outside Mr. Hartbustle's shop, and her surprise evaporated, leaving anger in its stead. "How dare you speak such slander? Mr. Hartbustle is a kind man and a wonderful sorcerer!"

"No, Miss Bennet. Once again you are mistaken. Mr. Hartbustle is not what he seems. Whatever the Coven may say to the contrary, I work, as I always have, for the good of mankind. What cause have I ever given you to believe otherwise?"

"You have a dangerous book, *Blood Magicks*, hidden by the Palimpsest Spell," Mary replied.

"My mother told me she thought you had seen that. Very impressive, Miss Bennet. But it is misguided of you to believe that the book's presence in my collection indicates anything specific about my practice of sorcery. Only a handful of spells in that book are dark in nature. The rest are purely beneficial. Moreover, I have liberated that book from a less judicious owner who sees only the power to be gained and not the good to be performed with it."

Mary paused, confused. Mr. Huntley had made a fine point. How could she offer the book as evidence of *his* deadliness when Mr. Hartbustle, whom she trusted and admired, had been searching for the same book? But no, she must not think this way. The Glastonbury Sorcerer would use every means to deceive her. Somewhere there must be a flaw in Mr.

Huntley's logic, and she would find it.

"You recoiled!" she cried.

"I beg your pardon, Miss Bennet?"

"When I took your arm to lead you in to dinner. I had a protection charm in my pocket, and you recoiled as soon as you touched me. Why else would you have such a reaction if not because you had intended me harm and my charm protected me?"

"There was a small pebble in my shoe. At the same instant that you took my arm, I shifted my weight directly onto the pebble. It was an unpleasant sensation that had nothing to do with you. But I did think I smelled hyssop and elderberries. It seems I was correct," replied Mr. Huntley.

"But…but what about the ship from India?" said Mary, her confidence wavering.

"Which ship from India?"

"The one that you attacked!"

"I have attacked no ship, Miss Bennet."

"But at the meeting—there was a report. Several members of the crew were found wandering on the beach, lost and severely beaten. The cargo had disappeared. Mr. Spottiswoode said that he suspected you were responsible because there were books about powerful Indian magic on board that you coveted."

Mr. Huntley shook his head. "I believe the entire meeting was probably staged for your benefit, Miss Bennet. Mr. Spottiswoode simply played his part," he said gently. "What else happened at that meeting?"

Mary thought for a moment. "Mr. Callan asked for volunteers to search for you in Glastonbury. Lady Vinton and Miss Clarkson responded."

"They never arrived in Glastonbury, Miss Bennet. I would have known had they set foot within twenty miles of my whereabouts. You are not the only sorcerer in Hertfordshire with a thorough knowledge of protection spells." He smiled again. "Did anything else happen that struck you in any way?"

Mary began to shake her head, but then remembered the strange outburst from poor Miss Clarkson. "The youngest one, Miss Clarkson, seemed particularly agitated about the missing books. She cried out, saying something like, 'It will not work without the book.' And then she clapped her hands over her mouth as though she had said something improper. She seemed so frightened, I could not help but pity her."

"And how did Mr. Hartbustle respond to her exclamation?"

Mary searched her memory. "He asked me not to mind her enthusiasm, I believe. Why do you ask?"

"It would seem that Miss Clarkson nearly revealed their actual business to you, Miss Bennet," replied Mr. Huntley. "You have seen the book to which she referred."

"Where?"

"In my parlor."

"Not *Blood Magicks*?"

"The very book. It contains a spell that would allow the Coven to gather all of the magic in the world for their own use, something they have been trying to accomplish for some time now. In the process they would draw power from every sorcerer and sorceress not protected from the spell, thus killing them without compunction."

Unable to believe what she had just heard, Mary shook her head violently. "No," she protested. "I cannot imagine that Mr. Hartbustle could ever do something so cruel, so horrid."

Mr. Huntley looked at her, an expression of kind concern on his face. "Ah, Miss Bennet, I understand. But I am afraid that your trust is misplaced. How shall I convince you?" He thought for a moment before continuing, "My father taught me that one might take the measure of a man by the company he chooses to keep. Tell me, Miss Bennet, at any time during that meeting or at any other time in the Coven's presence did you experience misgivings?"

Mary's eyes widened. How could he know? "Yes," she said softly.

"What kind of man surrounds himself with such people?"

The same thought had occurred to Mary, but she had dismissed it. "But Mr. Hartbustle was so kind to me. It was only the others…" Mary dropped her eyes to her lap. Had she betrayed the Coven? What might they do to her? What would Mr. Hartbustle think? The afternoon was taking a turn she had not anticipated.

"Yes, he is masterful at hiding behind his mask of goodness. I remember the first time I met Mr. Hartbustle. I liked him instantly. He seemed such a sweet soul."

At the sadness in Mr. Huntley's voice, Mary looked up, surprised. He gazed into the fire, far away in his thoughts. They sat in that attitude for several minutes, the sound of rain filling the silence. Finally Mr. Huntley sighed. "I must apologize to you, Miss Bennet. I had no idea that you entertained such suspicions about me. Had I known, I would not have hesitated to do whatever I must to dispel them." He looked at Mary, his blue eyes soft and warm. "Miss

Bennet, would you do a favor for me?"

"What is it?" she replied, her uncertainty making her shiver. He seemed so vulnerable that her heart began to ache for him.

"Would you answer a question for me?"

"I shall do my best."

"Your instincts provided you with certain useful information about the Bloomsbury Coven's members. I would like you to consult them about me. When you close your eyes and ask, deep down inside yourself, whether or not I am an evil man, what is the answer that comes to you?"

Mary considered his request for a moment, wondering if he was trying to trick her, but then she closed her eyes and asked herself the question. What she found when she examined her deepest thoughts and feelings startled her: Mary discovered that she felt very fond of Mr. Huntley. Despite her fears, despite any misgivings she may have had about his identity, she realized that she anticipated seeing Mr. Huntley with eagerness whenever the opportunity arose. Putting those unsettling feelings aside, she continued to ask herself whether or not she believed he could be an evil man. When she had reached her conclusion, she looked into Mr. Huntley's lovely blue eyes, and smiled. "No," she said, "you are not evil. If I have ever felt any misgivings while in your presence, I am sure now that they were born from an imagination under the influence of your enemies."

"I thank you," he replied.

"But Mr. Huntley, if you are not as the Coven describes you, then why have you taken such an interest in me?"

"As I told you before, Miss Bennet, I should have

thought that was obvious."

"Not to me, Mr. Huntley," said Mary.

"I have been intrigued by you since the night of the ball at Mr. Darcy's house in London. I meant what I said a moment ago—you performed that spell flawlessly. All three of the spells were perfect. I know that you saw me and that you understood that I had seen what you were doing. After our silent interaction, I spoke to Darcy about you. I am sorry to say that Mr. Darcy's description did not flatter you, but I saw something in you he could not: great power.

"After that evening I followed you from time to time, even after you learned about the Corridor of Doors, which, I admit, presented some difficulties as there are few hiding places in that stone passageway. At any rate, I saw you visit Mr. Hartbustle's shop on a number of occasions, including one in which I believe you caught me watching you. I also happened to be outside the shop the day you attended that meeting, observing from a distance as the other sorcerers entered and then waiting for you to leave. I should have spoken to you then, but I did not know how to approach you. Instead I sent you that book about Indian magic. Admittedly, it was an enigmatic gesture, but I wanted you to read it so that you would know what the Bloomsbury Coven fought for. I already had proof that you are a powerful sorceress. I hoped that I could recruit you for my purposes."

Mary felt the familiar blush creeping up her neck and staining her cheeks. She looked out the window to hide her embarrassment. The rain had stopped and the sun had made a watery appearance. A thought nagged at Mary.

"How did you know to send me your first book,

Mr. Huntley?" she asked.

"I did not send it. It was a simple mistake. I required an unmarked copy of *An Introductory Guide* for the revisions I wished to make before releasing the new edition, but it never arrived. In its stead I received a book entitled *A Sicilian Romance* accompanied by a short note addressed to a Miss Mary Bennet, suggesting several additional titles that may be of interest. When I discovered that the young woman performing those spells at the ball was the very same Miss Mary Bennet, reader of novels, I knew immediately that you had not only read the book, but had also learned to work the spells. It takes a rare talent to accomplish such a task alone." He smiled.

Mary returned his smile. The clock on the mantel chimed. "Oh dear!" she cried. "I had no idea it had grown so late! My mother will be worried about me." She leapt to her feet.

"Of course," said the vicar, rising with her. "Shall I accompany you to Longbourn? Perhaps if your mother learns where you have been, her mind will find some relief."

Mary smiled. "My arriving home with you would give my mother an inexhaustible topic of conversation. But to spare my father, I believe I shall manage on my own."

"Well then, Miss Bennet, may I at least see you out?"

"Of course, Mr. Huntley," she said taking his arm.

At the door Mary hesitated and then turned to face the vicar. "Mr. Huntley," she said, "I must apologize for my dreadful assumptions."

"You are forgiven, Miss Bennet. I hope you realize that we have much more to discuss and that the opportunity to do so presents itself with haste."

"As do I, Mr. Huntley," Mary replied before hurrying away.

The walk home passed without her notice, for she was deep in thought about the afternoon's events. Mary was relieved that the confrontation had taken such a surprising turn, as she had feared the worst. Although she believed Mr. Huntley was not a danger to her or to her family, she still could not bring herself to consider that Mr. Hartbustle might be. She had trusted the kindly old gentleman; he had never given her reason to do otherwise. And then she froze mid-step. The letter she had written to Mr. Hartbustle had betrayed Mr. Huntley's location. Would that put him in grave danger? Worried, she resumed her walk at a much quicker pace. She would have to write another letter when she got home. She just hoped it would not be too late.

CHAPTER XIII

*M*ary arrived home without exciting anyone's notice. Relieved, she hurried to her room to complete the unpleasant letter to Mr. Huntley. Although she agonized for a full quarter of an hour over how to phrase her betrayal, however, she could not bring herself to confess in writing what she had done. Finally, she settled on composing a short note urging Mr. Huntley to meet her in the churchyard early the next morning. Her circumstances prevented her from worrying about the request's general impropriety. Indeed, grave danger stood between her and the dictates of good manners. When she finished writing the note, she rang for Sarah and once more directed the maid to post the letter observing the utmost secrecy.

"Sarah, I realize I have placed you in an uncomfortable position by requiring so much concealment," Mary said as the girl turned to leave. "I wish I could divulge to you my reasons, but my current circumstances prevent me from doing so."

Sarah gave a bewildered nod, but made no reply. Taking the note she shuffled out of the room.

When the door closed and Sarah's footsteps had receded down the hall, Mary sighed. "Poor girl," she said. "I must find another way to communicate. I cannot continue to rely on her discretion." Then, consulting the small clock on her mantle, she determined that she had just enough time before she was expected downstairs for dinner to cast a protection spell over the vicarage. She could not be certain of its overall efficacy, but she wished to do something to assuage the guilt she felt for betraying Mr. Huntley to the Bloomsbury Coven. When she finished the spell, she dressed for dinner and returned downstairs.

That evening and the following morning passed without event, and after breakfast, Mary slipped out of the house. No note had arrived from the vicarage, by Mary's request. Nevertheless, she hurried to the churchyard to meet Mr. Huntley. She reached the assigned location a few moments early. The day was dark and overcast, and Mary shivered inside her pelisse. But a deeper cold troubled her as well. How would Mr. Huntley react when he discovered what she had done? Could he forgive her betrayal?

When Mr. Huntley strode into sight, Mary's heartbeat quickened and a smile formed on her lips despite her anxiety. Catching sight of her, Mr. Huntley returned her smile.

"Good morning, Miss Bennet!"

"Good morning, Mr. Huntley."

"Oh my, you are cold! Let us go in to my study. We may find shelter and speak without intrusion."

Mary hesitated. "Is your mother at home?" she

asked.

"Yes, Miss Bennet, although she will not interrupt us. But for propriety's sake, I shall not close the door."

Reassured, Mary agreed and allowed Mr. Huntley to lead her into the vicarage. As it had the previous day, a fire burned in the study's hearth. Lamps were lit against the gloom, casting their soft glow around the room. Mary was pleased to return to the comfort of Mr. Huntley's study.

"Now, what was the urgent matter you wished to discuss, Miss Bennet?" asked Mr. Huntley once they had settled themselves.

"I am not sure how to soften the blow, Mr. Huntley," Mary said, "so I shall have to come straight to the point. I have betrayed you."

"In what way?"

"Shortly after my mother and I ate dinner at the vicarage, I wrote a letter to Mr. Hartbustle informing him of my suspicions that you were the Glastonbury Sorcerer. I used as my proof the presence of *Blood Magicks* in your collection, hidden as it is by the Palimpsest Spell."

What followed was the longest half a minute of silence that Mary hoped ever to endure. Finally Mr. Huntley spoke. "I would have liked more time to prepare, but I suppose there is some relief to be found in the end of this dreadful wait."

"I am so terribly sorry, Mr. Huntley," whispered Mary. "Please forgive me."

"Oh, Miss Bennet, the time would have come sooner or later; I have been running from the Coven for so many years now. I am at fault for not simply explaining myself to you."

Mary shook her head and said, "No, Mr. Huntley. You must understand my folly. I wanted to believe myself in the middle of a grand intrigue. I have longed for adventure since I began reading novels of the sort you received by mistake. My life appeared rather dull by contrast to the trials faced by those heroines whose stories I loved so much. I have not had much enjoyment or adventure in my life, Mr. Huntley," Mary confessed. "But then your book arrived, and I went to London and met Mr. Hartbustle who introduced me to the Bloomsbury Coven. When I learned of your existence, it seemed, finally, I was at the center of something larger than my little life. I was terrified to be sure, but also thrilled. And now I have put you and your mother in terrible danger. All because of my foolishness and my gullible belief in Mr. Hartbustle." Mary wiped away a tear that had strayed down her cheek.

"My dear Miss Bennet!" cried Mr. Huntley. "You must not despair! I have placed powerful protection spells around all that I hold dear. I have time to prepare for the battle that comes."

"I wish to help you fight, Mr. Huntley," said Mary.

"No, Miss Bennet. I cannot let you put yourself in harm's way. I could never forgive myself should something happen to you."

"And I shall never forgive myself should any harm come to *you*, Mr. Huntley," Mary replied.

"But you have no idea what you would face."

"Then teach me. Please. I want to know." Mary was resolute and would brook no arguments. "How did you become a member of the Coven, Mr. Huntley?"

"I suppose Mr. Hartbustle told you," he said.

Mary nodded.

"Well," he began, gazing into the fire as though embarrassed to face Mary. "I was in my second year at Oxford, young and easily influenced, when I met Michael Callan, a fellow divinity student. We became friends and soon enough discovered our *other* shared interest. Callan had met Mr. Hartbustle in London the previous summer. He seemed to worship the man, so when I had the opportunity to make Mr. Hartbustle's acquaintance, I took it. Callan had piqued my curiosity, and I wished to see this great sorcerer for myself. I was not disappointed. Mr. Hartbustle was, as Callan insisted, not only a brilliant sorcerer, but also a terribly kind man. Or so he appeared.

"Soon enough we developed a close friendship. I had lost my father suddenly the year before, and I still grieved for him. Mr. Hartbustle became a surrogate father for me."

"Mr. Hartbustle told me he considered you almost his son," Mary interrupted gently. "He seemed genuinely moved by the memory."

Mr. Huntley looked up sharply, eyebrows raised. "Mr. Hartbustle is a consummate actor, Miss Bennet."

"I do not believe he was acting in that moment, Mr. Huntley. There was something so vulnerable about how he said it, as if his heart had broken."

"Perhaps you are right, Miss Bennet. I have to believe that he was once a kind man and that the darkness in him came later. He certainly demonstrated only the most amiable nature to me. At least at first. But I am getting ahead of myself.

"Later that year Mr. Hartbustle invited me to join the Bloomsbury Coven. First there was a trial to pass, which I performed willingly. It was my task to find a missing book. I am sure you can guess which one."

Mary thought for a moment. "*Blood Magicks*," she whispered.

"Yes. Specifically the sixteenth century translation into English of the original book. Mr. Hartbustle claimed that the Coven wished to destroy it, but the truth was far more upsetting. Only two copies of that translation had ever been made. One had been stolen from its first guardian and destroyed. The other copy had disappeared, but rumors of its continuing existence persisted. I was to find that lost book. When I began my trial I did not know that most of the Coven believed I was embarking on a fool's errand. But to their surprise, I returned after three months of searching with the very book they desired. Much to *my* surprise, I learned eventually that the Coven, as I told you yesterday, intended a very different future for the book. Naturally they were overjoyed at my success. But something evil lurked beneath that joy, and even before I discovered their plan, I knew I had made a terrible mistake."

Mr. Huntley paused and gazed out of the window, a shadow passing across his handsome features. Mary could not bear the sadness and shame she saw expressed on his face, so she reached out and took his hand in hers. He continued to stare out the window, but squeezed her fingers gently. A moment later he resumed speaking, her hand still held lightly in his.

"After that, although I maintained every appearance of being a loyal member of the Coven, I began plotting to remove the book from their possession. I knew that such an act would set off a chain of events that could lead to my death, but I felt I had no choice. The book had been removed from this world for a reason, and by retrieving it and placing it in the Coven's hands, I had unleashed something awful. It was my responsibility to right that great wrong."

"Mr. Huntley," Mary asked, "how would removing the book from their possession stop them from acting? Could they not have learned the spells and used them without the book?"

"An excellent question, Miss Bennet. But the book keeps its secrets. Woven into its design is an ancient magic that prevents a sorcerer from remembering the book's spells even after he has just performed them."

Mary marveled at the powerful magic that the book must contain.

"So you see, Miss Bennet, I had to remove it. During the agonizing months of my scheme, I stumbled across the Palimpsest Spell, which changed the course of my actions. Previously I had every intention of destroying the book, but now I could hide it. As I told you yesterday, the book contains much magic that is useful. The healing spells alone atone for the darker magic in its pages. When I had perfected the Palimpsest Spell—no easy feat, I assure you—I knew it was time to act. First I created a false book with a glamour that I had adapted to maintain its appearances without my presence. Then I broke into Mr. Hartbustle's shop, retrieved the book, and left the false copy behind. As I had no idea how much time I would have before they discovered the forgery, I fled home and worked the Palimpsest Spell on the copy of my father's book, which you saw in the vicarage.

"Fortunately, by the time they discovered the false book, I was ensconced in Glastonbury. I drew on the power of the place to construct barrier spells, allowing none of the Coven within a twenty-mile radius of the parish where I served as vicar without considerable harm to them and without setting off an alarm that would notify me of their presence. I also modified the Palimpsest Spell: with my death, the book I have hidden disappears forever."

They sat in silence for a moment as Mary absorbed the story. She was impressed by his improvements to already difficult spells and hoped to learn more about them when the more pressing matter of their imminent danger had been resolved. But his story had raised at least one question for her.

"Mr. Huntley, why did you speak so favorably about the Coven in your book?"

"I wrote about them before I met them, but once I knew what they were, I did not correct what I had written because I could not simply tell the world the truth about the most famous and powerful Coven in England without concrete evidence of their wrongdoing. Despite my feelings and their desire for the book, they had committed no crimes during my time as a member. But now I have in my possession the evidence I require. I can now reveal the monstrous truth about the Bloomsbury Coven."

Mr. Huntley rose and walked over to his desk, took a small key from a chain around his neck, and unlocked the bottom drawer from which he removed a piece of parchment yellowed with age. Without speaking he handed the parchment to Mary. She read it in silence.

Derestt Frende,

I wryte to you in feare for my Lyfe. I hav discouvered the Truth abowt the moste wyked Blumesbury Covenne. They practis the moste Terrifying Magickes nown to Mankinde. I have witnessed wyth these, myne own eyes, the practis of Blode Magick from the Indes strictly for the Gaine and Profit of the members of the Coven.

The leder, a Cuning and Devylish man, puts forthe a Joculare and Kyndly Fase. But I hav seen his Tru Natur lurcking beneath the Maske he wears. He is nothing less than a Deville. I must confess that I mayd selfish use of his wicked character for myne own gayn when I wrote "The Tragicall Histtory of the Lyfe and Deth of Docktor Faustes." Yet when the play's tru inspiration is understood by the Covenne, my life will be forfyt, for that devill Hartbustle wil not want to be expos'd so.

Furthermor, befor I left the Covenne Forever, I stole the sorce of their Wicked Blode Magicks, an anktient book from the Indes. They have discovered the Truthe about its disaperance and Shall claym their Vengeance agaynst me.

My dere Frende, I kno I have no recorse to safety. I simply wish it to be knowne that if I dy in the coming weks that I was murdered in cold blode by the Blumesbury Covenne.

I remaine your Humbel Servant,

C. Marlowe

When Mary finished reading, she looked up in

amazement at Mr. Huntley. Several questions fought for place in her mind. "This is remarkable!" she exclaimed. "Where did you find it? What did he mean about 'that devil Hartbustle?' Surely he cannot mean *our* Mr. Hartbustle!"

"I do not know if he means our Mr. Hartbustle. The Coven was founded by *a* Hartbustle. However, I never learned more about its origins than that. Spells exist that slow the body's aging, and Mr. Hartbustle could perform them, but that is speculation.

"As for the letter, I believe it was written to Sir Thomas Walsingham, a patron of Mr. Marlowe's. I found it in a book I bought from the estate about a year ago. I have no evidence that Sir Thomas provided any aid to his friend. History certainly has not been kind in its portrait of Mr. Marlowe's death in Deptford. Given this letter, I believe something more suspicious than a drunken brawl led to Mr. Marlowe's demise. The man who stabbed the playwright, a Mr. Ingram Frizer, claimed he merely defended himself from an attack. I am not certain that it has any significance, but Sir Thomas was also patron to Mr. Frizer. More important is the fact that both men enjoyed membership in the Bloomsbury Coven. From this fact I have concluded that the Coven planned Marlowe's death and then circulated the story we know in order to obscure their guilt."

Mary let out her breath in a long sigh, feeling her head swim with all that she had learned. She stared into the fire, wondering what to ask next. Finally, feeling Mr. Huntley's eyes upon her, she looked up and met his gaze. "You must allow me to help you fight the Coven, Mr. Huntley. I knew what they were, and yet I continued to believe my misgivings stemmed solely from my imagination."

"No, Miss Bennet, I—"

"Mr. Huntley, please. You said yourself that I am powerful and that you had hoped to enlist me in your cause. If you do not, I shall strike out on my own, so you may as well agree to teach me to fight."

Mr. Huntley sighed. "I suppose I have no choice then, do I?"

"No, you do not."

Mr. Huntley nodded, resigned.

"Good. So, Mr. Huntley, what do we do now?"

"Now you go home and read, my brave Miss Bennet. For tomorrow we prepare for battle."

CHAPTER XIV

*M*ary departed Mr. Huntley's study carrying several books, having promised to pass the night in study. They had agreed it would be best to meet early the next morning and in some place where they might work in secret. Mary suggested a small, sheltered clearing in Longbourn's wilderness. After repeated assurances from her that the other residents of the house avoided the less cultivated areas of their grounds, Mr. Huntley agreed. At the end of the lane, Mary turned and looked back toward the vicarage. Mr. Huntley stood in the doorway, his handsome face etched with lines of worry. Hoping to dispel his distress, Mary called to him, "Please, Mr. Huntley, do not concern yourself so. I am quite resolved on my course. Nothing can dissuade me. Best to return to your study and begin reading."

"As you say, Miss Bennet," he replied. "Until the morning, then."

Mary nodded and then hurried away lest he change his mind.

That evening, equal measures of apprehension and exhilaration prevented Mary from succumbing to the temptation of her soft bed. Instead, she remained at her desk, working late into the night. Before opening any of the books lent to her by Mr. Huntley, she made a list of the spells she had already mastered, noting how each might prove useful in a magical battle. Mary was pleased by the list's length and gratified by the many protection spells her misplaced fear of the Glastonbury Sorcerer had prompted her to learn. They would provide much-needed defense against the very people who had encouraged that fear. Absent from her list, however, were spells more specifically designed for combat.

Seeking to address that deficiency, Mary turned to the first book stacked on her desk, a thick volume entitled *Battle Magic*. With keen interest, she opened it.

> *It is an unfortunate but universally known truth that sorcerers are not exempt from the darker qualities of human nature, including the propensity for waging senseless wars born of greed or ignorance. Centuries of history have proved that mages are no different from other mortals and will erupt into war against each other with little need for provocation. This tendency has led to the creation of a vast and startling array of battle spells. The business of this book is to catalogue and describe such spells.*
>
> *For the reader's ease, the spells have been arranged according to the following categories: Protection and Defensive Deflection; Traps, Ambush, and Detention; and Wounding and Killing.*

Mary paused, troubled by the notion that engaging in battle may force her to inflict mortal wounds. Yet, she wondered, would the members of the Bloomsbury Coven hesitate so? Would they succumb to such squeamishness? She was certain they would not. A cold thrill passed through her as she understood the enormity of her situation—in a few days' time she might have to face her own mortality. Mary shuddered and then banished those thoughts. She would have time enough later for such worries. Thus resolved, she returned to work.

A quick glance through the book's first chapters told her she already knew many of those spells, so she turned to "Traps, Ambushes, and Detention," where a spell for throwing fire caught her eye. It appeared simple enough, despite its florid incantation, so she stood in the center of her room, held out her hand, and chanted, "Source of life, dancing flame, bringer of strife, I call your name." Although she knew the incantation's poetry lacked taste, she enjoyed uttering it and was pleased by the prompt appearance in her hand of a ball of flame. "From my hand move fast and true, toward my enemy and there burn through." She watched, amazed, as the ball of fire darted across her room. Instead of landing in the hearth as she had expected, it dropped onto the braided hearthrug. For a moment Mary stood frozen, shocked by her failure. But seeing the flames licking at the wool and beginning to spread toward her, she picked up the vase sitting on her vanity table, removed the flowers, and extinguished the fire before it could spread.

"My goodness! I shall have to observe more care with my targets! Perhaps it is best not to practice this one indoors," she whispered. And making the appropriate notes about the spell, she returned to the book to study. Several hours passed without further incident as Mary added more spells to her list, including a simple spell for dousing small fires, until finally, exhausted from her work, she collapsed onto her bed and fell into a restless sleep.

Strange visions assailed her as she slid from wakefulness into slumber. Shapes and sounds surrounded her, but she could not discern them. Suddenly she stood on the edge of a great precipice in the midst of swirling clouds and a howling wind that threatened to knock her over. Despite a deep foreboding, she felt compelled to look down into the void gaping beneath her. There she saw a dark, pulsing mass, which seethed with energy and power. An aching hunger prompted her to stretch out her hand. If she could touch just a fraction of that power, her hunger might be satisfied. Though the shapeless figure drew her incessantly, she could not approach it. Wracked by despair, she fell to her knees even as she continued to reach. Then she was falling down through endless space, her limbs scrambling to right her, panic coursing through her.

Mary startled awake. For a moment she lay in her bed, quivering. But slowly the morning light poured over her, and she realized that she was safe in her room. It had only been a dream. Yet that insatiable hunger, that craving carving out a space inside her, still held her in its grip even as the dream receded from her memory. What caused that deep desire? What might that dream portend? Mary was not certain that she wished to know. Still shaking, she rose from her bed, crossed over to her basin, and splashed cold water on her face. Slowly the longing faded. After dressing in a simple gown, she sat at her desk to review her notes from the previous evening. Satisfied that she was prepared for the morning's activities, she snuck out of her room and paused by the kitchen where she purloined two breakfast buns. Then she hurried to meet Mr. Huntley.

When she arrived in the small copse, she found Mr. Huntley waiting for her on a stone bench. He smiled at her approach. "This is indeed a perfectly hidden spot for our practice, Miss Bennet."

"It is lovely, is it not?" she replied, handing him a bun. He thanked her with a bow. "Since my sisters have left home," she continued, "it has been all but abandoned. I come here in good weather to enjoy the peace of this place. Further along there is a stream. If you listen carefully you may hear it. At this time of year it runs with more force."

They stood in silence for a moment, both in attitudes of great attention.

"Yes, there it is. It sounds lovely," said Mr. Huntley. "But Miss Bennet," he continued, examining her, "you look as though you slept not a wink. Is it wise for you to be out here this morning? Should you not be in your bed?"

"There is nothing for you to worry about, Mr. Huntley. I worked late into the night, and when I did finally fall into bed, I had a very strange dream."

"Indeed? What made it strange?"

Mary recounted what she could remember of the dream, many of its details having fled with the dawn. For some reason, perhaps embarrassment, she could not bring herself to tell Mr. Huntley about the deep desire overtaking her in the face of the great power. "I suppose it was a fancy born of a tired mind," she concluded.

"I am not sure that I would say as much, Miss Bennet. Dreams may indeed mean nothing, but sometimes they reveal much about the dreamer, or they may serve as windows to the future. Should you recall any further details, please alert me. But in the meanwhile, we must begin our work. What have you learned?"

Dismissing the guilt she felt for omitting an important detail of her dream, Mary thought about which spell to demonstrate. A moment later, a ball of flame danced in her palm.

"Impressive, Miss Bennet!"

Pleased, Mary uttered the words that sent the ball of fire directly toward a twig lying in the path. She let it burn for just a moment before dousing it. Proud of her accomplishment, Mary smiled, but required a short rest after the effort of calling and then quenching the fire. She lowered herself onto the stone bench. The night before her elation had masked the spell's difficulty.

"A marvelous choice," said Mr. Huntley. "And executed with perfection."

"Thank you, Mr. Huntley," Mary replied. "And now you must demonstrate something for me."

"With pleasure, Miss Bennet, but first you must move back a few feet if you please." As Mary complied with his request, Mr. Huntley placed a doll on the bench. Stepping to Mary's side, he whispered a spell. A moment later a mist rose up out of the ground, surrounded the doll, and then vanished, taking the doll with it.

Mary was all astonishment. Naturally she had expected an impressive performance of magic from

Mr. Huntley, but nothing could have prepared her for the firsthand observation of his skills. "Mr. Huntley," Mary breathed, "To make something vanish! The effort that must require, yet you stand there as though unaffected!"

"I have had many years to practice, Miss Bennet," replied Mr. Huntley. "Over that time I have experimented with methods to make magic less fatiguing. I strive to achieve the utmost ease, having learned from several mages in India that without ease one may become so deranged by magic as to become morally corrupted. I believe something of that sort has happened to Mr. Hartbustle. Dark magic exacts an even greater toll on the sorcerer, disturbing something essential within him—or her—to the point of permanent alteration. But even when practicing the most wholesome magic, we must preserve our energy to protect ourselves. For that reason I waste little time with incantations and foreign languages. The fewest words spoken in one's native language should always suffice. Breathe steadily and concentrate. You need expend no more effort than that. Would you like to try?"

Mary replied with a vigorous nod of her head.

"Excellent. I suspected as much. Now, stand over here while I find something for you to send into the mists. Ah, this will do quite nicely." Mr. Huntley set a large rock on the bench and moved back to Mary's side. "Listen first to the original incantation—"

"But will that not call the mists?" Mary asked.

Mr. Huntley smiled patiently. "Not if I have no intention behind the words."

"Of course," Mary said, blushing. "Please continue."

"Nameless ones I entreat you. Shapeless ones I call upon you. Bind my enemies with your breath. Take my enemies from this realm." Mr. Huntley paused. "Far more words than are necessary," he said. "By the time I finish the incantation, my enemy could easily have moved beyond my reach, so instead I have condensed it. Observe." Mr. Huntley took a deep breath, fixed his eyes on the rock, and said, "Bind and remove." The rock disappeared. "Fewer words translates to more concentrated power, Miss Bennet."

Mary tried to hide her disappointment. She knew that the spell was as effective as it had been before, but there was something enchanting about speaking even silly incantations. As though sensing her feelings, Mr. Huntley said, "I know it may seem less thrilling, Miss Bennet, but precision in magic is terribly important and in the battle we face, necessary for our survival."

Mary nodded. "Indeed, Mr. Huntley. I trust your direction."

They passed another hour in this manner, taking time to adapt the spells Mary had discovered to Mr. Huntley's mode of practice. Mary was pleased both by how much simpler the magic became and by how much more power she could channel with each spell. When Mary succeeded in blasting an entire shrubbery from their path, Mr. Huntley beamed. "Wonderful, Miss Bennet! And I believe that is enough effort for one morning. You should return home and rest, for tomorrow we must continue."

Upon returning home Mary discovered her mother waiting for her in the drawing room.

"Where have you been, Mary?" demanded Mrs.

Bennet.

"The morning was so lovely that I decided to pass it by wandering in the wilderness," Mary replied.

Her mother raised her eyebrows. "Hill tells me that you were seen in the kitchen this morning. In the kitchen! Mary Bennet, whatever could have brought you there?"

"I—I was unable to sleep, Mama," she began, "but I was hungry. I did not wish to disturb the servants, so I went to the kitchen to find something to take with me on my walk."

Mrs. Bennet shook her head. "I shall never understand you, Mary. What has gotten into you? You have become so…so *unusual*. You always were *different* from your sisters, but you have become such a mystery."

"Mama, I have no explanation at all. Perhaps you simply see more of me than you did before. I do not believe I have altered so very much. But my sisters are no longer here for comparison," Mary said, shrugging away her hurt feelings. "At any rate, I find that I have grown quite tired and should like to retire to my room to rest."

"I can make no objection, but I request that you join us for dinner this afternoon," said her mother.

"I shall," Mary replied, taking her leave. When she regained the sanctuary of her room, Mary sat down at her desk and stared out the window, lost in thought. Mary's mother had always doted on her other daughters, especially Lydia, leaving Mary largely unnoticed. Although she had tried to take solace in her books and music, she had longed for her mother's regard. Now, the only daughter still at home, Mary resented her mother's awkward and sometimes cruel attention. She longed for the days when she could slip undetected through the house. Sighing, Mary returned to her work, knowing that such concerns paled before the threat she faced from the Bloomsbury Coven.

The next few days followed a similar pattern. Mary read late into the night and then met Mr. Huntley in the morning to practice what she had studied and to learn new spells. On the third morning, as they rested, Mary asked Mr. Huntley about the other members of the Coven. "I was granted only one opportunity to observe them," she explained, "so I should like to learn more about them. What are they like, Mr. Huntley? Do they share Mr. Hartbustle's power?"

"My association with them did not last long enough to discover all that I might have about their powers. Moreover they were circumspect in what they chose to share with me. I learned very quickly that questions of a personal nature were not tolerated. But eager as I was to belong in the Coven, I observed everyone closely whenever I could. From those observations I ascertained a great deal.

"The most powerful member of the Coven, Mr. Hartbustle, will prove the most difficult to defeat, but I imagine you could have guessed that yourself." Mr. Huntley paused, gathering his thoughts. "Lady Vinton is fearless, which makes her a dangerous adversary. I once witnessed an encounter between her and a wolf that left me astonished. She smiled as she fought the beast, dainty yet ruthless in her magical attacks. The poor creature died a painful and pitiful death. But she is also a terribly vain woman, proud to a fault of her red hair, beautiful gowns, and jewels. That is a weakness we can exploit."

Mary nodded, remembering how Lady Vinton had moved her plump hands to show off her rings. She had thought the woman silly, but then had felt something of the ferocity that Mr. Huntley described seething underneath Lady Vinton's cloying politeness.

"Mrs. Post," continued Mr. Huntley, "always treated me as a friend and an equal. It was she who showed me the Vanishing Spell I taught you a few days ago. I have no doubt that should she learn about our lesson, she would consider it a serious betrayal. She is a jealous woman, easily moved to anger, which clouds her judgment and causes her to act rashly."

"To me she appeared terribly cold," said Mary. "I shuddered whenever I came under her scrutiny, for it left me feeling out of sorts and unsafe." Mary stopped, apprehension clouding her features.

"What is it, Miss Bennet?" asked Mr. Huntley, his voice softened by concern.

"A memory," Mary replied, and after a moment's pause, she recounted the disconcerting events of her first introduction to Mrs. Post, shuddering as she recalled the cold that had frozen her in place.

"It would seem you fell victim to a spell of Mrs. Post's invention. She calls it the Frozen Enemy Spell. Without dismissing the danger she poses, I must say that I always admired her forthrightness. She never favors spells burdened by flourishes and foreign languages. Her magic is always clean and precise. And terrifying," he added.

"Yes, it was terrifying," said Mary. "I wonder how long she would have held me there had it not been for Mr. Hartbustle's interference?"

"Experience tells me that she would have enjoyed your discomfort for as long as was practical for her.

She will no doubt rely on that spell in battle, for it can be applied to more than one enemy at a time. As you discovered, it is remarkably effective. But there is a simple counter spell. Envision yourself in the center of a circle made of ice. Then imagine a crack developing in the ice as you utter the command 'Melt.' If your intention is strong enough, you should be able to destroy her spell. But I will do my utmost to protect you from her."

"You have already done a great deal to that end, Mr. Huntley," said Mary, coloring at the strong emotion suddenly rushing through her.

Mr. Huntley smiled. "I hope so, Miss Bennet," he said, gazing at her warmly. Mary, a lovely fluttering feeling in her stomach, gazed back. A moment passed as they stood looking at each other. Without a word, Mr. Huntley reached out and touched Mary's face, giving it the gentlest of caresses.

At her furious blush he dropped his hand. "Y-yes, well, I, I—" Mr. Huntley stuttered. "I supposed there is more to say. About the Coven, I mean."

"I believe so, Mr. Huntley," replied Mary, equally discomposed.

"Where was I? Oh, yes, Miss Clarkson. Peculiar young woman. Never trusted me. But I imagine she trusts no humans, save for Mr. Hartbustle. She has an uncanny gift for calling and controlling beasts. No matter the creature, they obey her every wish. Even dragons, the most ferocious of magical creatures, behave like lap dogs with Miss Clarkson."

"Dragons? But surely those exist only in children's stories, Mr. Huntley!" cried Mary.

"Indeed they do not, Miss Bennet. Dragons, griffins, manticores, banshees, and a host of other fantastic beasts are all very real. But one must know where to find them and how to call them, which, I am afraid, must be a lesson for another day."

"Of course," said Mary. "And I look forward to it. But you were telling me about Miss Clarkson."

"Precisely. Her years of working with these creatures have had a profoundly altering effect on her. You see, Miss Bennet, whenever a sorcerer has dealings with such beings, he or she takes on certain of their characteristics, which often linger even after contact has ceased. Repeated interactions lead to physical and emotional distortions, as when a sorcerer employs dark magic."

"And that is her weakness?"

"No, I am afraid those distortions make her a formidable foe. Recklessness is her weakness. She will pursue her quarry beyond the bounds of good sense. Many were the times that Mr. Hartbustle had to employ healing spells to mend her broken bones and to soothe her scorches."

Mary required a moment to reconcile this information about Miss Clarkson with the different impression of the young woman she had gotten from the meeting. Miss Clarkson had seemed such a timid creature that Mary had been inspired to pity her. But influenced by Mr. Huntley's account, Mary hardened her heart against Miss Clarkson.

"And the gentlemen? What knowledge do you have of them?" Mary asked.

"I have never made the acquaintance of the stout one that I saw exiting Mr. Hartbustle's shop. What is he called?"

"Mr. Spottiswoode."

"He must have joined the Coven after I fled. But

Michael Callan was once my friend, so I am well acquainted with his faults. His competence extends only so far as to allow him to pass his trial for entering the Coven. Like many a mediocre sorcerer, he is fond of flourishes. He also insists upon using Latin for all of his spells. As a result of inaccurate pronunciation, he sometimes makes costly mistakes. I wasted many hours attempting to convince him to speak English. He refused to believe that it made a difference. Eventually I abandoned my attempts.

"In his favor, he has a talent for organizing people and delegating responsibilities, which makes him an effective leader, especially of sorcerers, who can be foolishly myopic at times. If we can—"

The sound of a twig snapping caused both Mr. Huntley and Mary to spring to their feet; eyes wide, they turned toward each other. How would Mary ever explain what she was doing in this secluded nook of the wilderness with Mr. Huntley? Or worse: what if their conversation had been overheard by an unscrupulous someone? They stood in an attitude of stillness for what seemed an eternity, but only the usual sounds of the woodland surrounded them. Mr. Huntley smiled sheepishly, and Mary exhaled, relieved. As they resumed their seats on the bench, however, a man's voice rang through the trees.

"At last, Huntley, we have found you."

CHAPTER XV

*F*ear seized Mary as several members of the Bloomsbury Coven strode into view. Mr. Huntley leapt to his feet, placing himself between the approaching sorcerers and Mary. Anxious to provide him with aid, she stood, breathing deeply to calm herself.

"I see you have a friend with you, Huntley," said Mr. Callan. "How lovely. Now if you would just run along and return home, Miss Bennet, you shall come to no harm."

"No," said Mary, stepping forward. "I will not leave Mr. Huntley." As she spoke, Mary glanced at the faces of the sorcerers surrounding them. Two of the Coven's members were missing: Mr. Hartbustle and Mr. Spottiswoode.

"So valiant," laughed Lady Vinton. "Is this your protector, Huntley?"

Mrs. Post cast a cold glance toward Lady Vinton, silencing her. "Listen to Mr. Callan, you silly girl," she said, turning her attention to Mary.

Clasping her hands behind her back to conceal her trembling, Mary faced Mrs. Post. "And why should I believe that you would not come after me as well?"

Mrs. Post sighed impatiently. "Because for some reason, which I cannot fathom, Mr. Hartbustle wishes you to remain untouched," she replied. "I knew the moment I looked at you that you do not belong in this Coven. You have no fortune, no notable parentage—you are nobody, Miss Bennet. Yet Mr. Hartbustle, who refuses to see reason, insisted upon preserving your security. He can be such a sentimental old fool."

"Enough," demanded Mr. Callan. "Huntley, I am sure you know very well what we want, so perhaps we may forgo the polite conversation."

"I beg your pardon, Callan, but I know nothing of what you desire. Please inform me," Mr. Huntley said, all politeness. Though amazed by Mr. Huntley's steadiness, Mary was mortified that he should hear Mrs. Post's insults to her dignity.

"The book!" cried Miss Clarkson, her placid features stretching into a hideous grimace. "You know that is why we have been hunting for you! Give us the book!"

"I am afraid I must disappoint you, Miss Clarkson," replied Mr. Huntley.

"Huntley, do you know what we do to sorcerers who defy us?" sneered Mrs. Post.

"In addition to spreading nasty rumors about them?" replied Mr. Huntley. "The Glastonbury Sorcerer indeed! I would have expected more from you, Mrs. Post. A hint of invention at the very least."

Mrs. Post's eyes narrowed. "That was a story for the girl, Huntley. It served its purpose. You will suffer far more than the insult of a silly name."

"Shall I be murdered as Christopher Marlowe was? He was an enemy of the Coven, too, was he not?"

Mrs. Post looked shaken, but Mr. Callan quickly spoke in her stead. "As a matter of fact, you shall. Of course your death will appear natural if untimely—"

"Then I have no reason to comply with your wishes," Mr. Huntley said before charging forward and exclaiming, "Now!"

Mary employed the first spell that came to her mind, conjuring a ball of fire and sending it straight toward the nearest enemy. It hit Lady Vinton, catching the lace of her sleeve. Lady Vinton stared at it for a moment before blowing on the flames in a desperate attempt to extinguish them. She shrieked as success evaded her, managing only to spread the fire up her arm to her shoulder where it set a stray red curl alight. "Help!" she screeched. "I'm burning. My hair! My beautiful hair!" Soon her head was a blaze of fire, and she disappeared into a ball of flame.

Mary watched, horrified by the knowledge that she had just killed someone. She was stunned that Lady Vinton had not tried anything more effective to stop the fire from consuming her, but then Mary remembered the woman's vanity. Mr. Huntley's assumption had proven correct. Yet the knowledge that Lady Vinton had let herself die did nothing to relieve Mary of the unpleasant feelings assailing her. With great effort, she resisted those feelings, tucking the truth of what she had done to the back of her mind so she would not have to face it. The battle had begun, and she had no time for guilt or dismay.

With Lady Vinton dispatched, Mary turned her attention to the rest of the field. She had been so intent upon her fire spell that she did not know what Mr. Huntley had done to the Coven. From the remaining members' reactions, Mary concluded that he had done *something*, for Mrs. Post, Mr. Callan, and Miss Clarkson were trapped in a confusion that distracted them long enough to allow Mary and Mr. Huntley to escape. Wasting no time, they turned and ran. As they reached the edge of the oldest, most overgrown section of the Longbourn wilderness, Mary heard Mr. Callan shout, "Miss Clarkson! The hounds! Call the hounds!"

Mary's curiosity proved stronger than her fear. Glancing back, she caught sight of something that arrested her movement as effectively as Mrs. Post's Frozen Enemy spell. Miss Clarkson stretched her arms toward the sky and opened her mouth. An eerie ululating erupted from the young woman whose visage had begun to change, stretching into something not quite human. Mary stood mesmerized, as from the earth sprang three enormous beasts whose well-muscled bodies and long legs were covered in matted grey fur. Mary thought the beasts resembled Irish wolfhounds, though far more hideous of aspect. Their open mouths revealed giant, sharp teeth, and their huge horns curled over sleek heads, reminding Mary of rams. "What are those?" she asked Mr. Huntley.

"Keep running!" panted Mr. Huntley, grabbing her hand and forcing her from her spot. "They are the Horned Hounds of Ufern," he breathed as they bounded over a shrubbery. "Miss Clarkson has grown quite powerful if she can control them. They are single-minded beasts, relentless when they have scented their prey."

"What shall do we do now?" Mary gasped, releasing his hand reluctantly to massage a pain in her side.

"*We* will do nothing. *I* will. There is no time for argument, Miss Bennet. I have trapped them behind a magical barrier, but they will find their way through it in a matter of moments. You hide in the first suitable place you find. Go. Continue to run. I will find you."

"No. I will not leave you," Mary said.

Mr. Huntley stopped, and Mary faced him, defiance shining from her eyes. "For what else have we been working than to defeat the Coven *together*?"

Another moment passed before Mr. Huntley acquiesced. "But you must fight from a distance," he insisted. "We did not finish preparing you, and I will not accept you placing yourself in an unnecessarily dangerous position."

"I believe, Mr. Huntley, that I am already *in* an unnecessarily dangerous position," Mary replied, pointing behind him.

He swung around. Miss Clarkson, Mrs. Post, and Mr. Callan had mounted the Hounds and were racing toward them. Again Mr. Huntley grabbed Mary's hand, muttering a protection spell that enveloped both of them in a golden glow. "This spell should repel the immediate attack, but they will have little difficulty breaking through it."

Mary drew a charm out of her pocket and handed it to Mr. Huntley. "Here, carry this charm; I added rowan berries to augment its power."

Mr. Huntley took the charm. Before he could stop her, Mary darted into the path of the Hounds. Miss Clarkson on her Hound led the others. "If you catch me, Miss Clarkson," Mary taunted, "perhaps I shall share with you what I know about the location of *Blood Magicks*." Then whispering the words of a spell she had learnt the night before, she caused a tree to fall in front of the Hounds, hindering their movement. She did not stay to see what happened. Instead, Mary bounded off the neatly kept footpath and into the wilder growth. She had to dodge around branches and bushes, but she succeeded in placing more distance between herself and the Hounds.

Nevertheless, when she looked back, she saw that Miss Clarkson still pursued her. Throwing away all notions of propriety, Mary gathered her skirts up around her thighs and ran faster, leading Miss Clarkson toward the brook that wound through the wilderness. It was a matter of pride to Mr. Bennet that their piece of woodland had grown so wild of late. Mary blessed her father silently for his unusual vanity as she leapt over a tree that had fallen across the narrow track. Soon she could see the brook ahead, its water glistening in the sunlight that streamed through the trees. Swollen by the season's heavy rain, the brook had gained considerable force, making it treacherous.

Mary heard Miss Clarkson growling behind her and ducked just in time to avoid a rock that sailed over her head. But the rock did not fall to the ground; instead, it circled back and resumed its pursuit of her. Panic gripped Mary, but then she remembered the first spell she had learned, and pointing toward the rock, she concentrated on diverting it. "Move there, please!" she cried. The rock wavered, but soon continued its flight toward her. "Move there, PLEASE!" Mary exclaimed, concentrating all her force on the rock. Finally it broke from its course and crashed into a tree.

Distracted by her victory, Mary did not see the roots jutting from the forest floor. Catching her toe on one of them, she tumbled to the ground. Behind her she heard a savage laugh. A chill ran through Mary's body at Miss Clarkson's transformation. No longer did she even resemble the young woman Mary had met in Mr. Hartbustle's shop. Instead something hideous careened toward her, crowing with triumph on the Hound's back. Gasping, Mary realized that Miss Clarkson had taken on the Hound's features. Her face had elongated, forming a snout; her open mouth revealed enormous fangs, and horns curled over her head. With a great effort Mary managed to return to her feet and jump aside just in time to avoid Miss Clarkson and the Hound as they bore down on her.

"Ah, Miss Bennet. I am terribly sorry to have to kill you, but it is for the good of the Coven," growled Miss Clarkson.

"I do so hope you know how to swim, Miss Clarkson," Mary replied.

Miss Clarkson looked up and saw the brook ahead of her just as the Hound came to an abrupt stop. She was thrown from the fearsome animal into the churning waters of the normally placid brook. Fortunately for Miss Clarkson, the rock with which her head came into contact had stunned her enough that she was insensible to the distress of drowning. As her head hit the rock, the Hound disappeared. Mary, alone by the brook, watched Miss Clarkson's body sink, amazed to see it disintegrate as it submerged.

Shaken, Mary dropped to the ground to catch her breath. But her rest was immediately interrupted by a blast located somewhere to her right. She jumped back to her feet and hurried in the direction of the noise. Another burst of sound told her that she was growing closer to it. A few steps more brought her to the edge of the wilderness where she saw Mr. Huntley battling the remaining members of the Coven. Mary rushed toward him. Her breaths came in gasps, and she felt a terrible burning in her right side, but on she ran.

Before she could enter the fray, she stopped. Mr. Huntley, chanting under his breath, had held up a hand to keep her back. She was shocked to see the bruises running up the left side of his face and the blood dripping from his knuckles. Nevertheless, she remained still, waiting for her chance to help him.

Mrs. Post and Mr. Callan, their Hounds nowhere in sight, hovered in the air, held alight by whatever spell Mr. Huntley was working. With a wave of his hand, he caused them to fly toward a small grove of poplars. They hit one of the trees with a thump and slid to the ground. "Wrap them," Mr. Huntley said, directing his gaze to the stunned sorcerers. In response, the tree's roots wound themselves around Mr. Callan and Mrs. Post, binding them in place.

Mr. Huntley bent over, gasping. Catching sight of Mary he shouted, "The mists, Miss Bennet! Call the mists."

Mary concentrated all her attention on imagining the mists rising from the ground as she chanted, "Bind and remove" over and over again. A tremor ran through the ground, nearly knocking Mary over, but she widened her stance and managed to stay on her feet. Finally mists began to rise around Mrs. Post and Mr. Callan.

"Huntley!" screeched Mrs. Post as the mist began to thicken around the imprisoned sorcerers. "You beast! How could you dare teach my spell to this girl?"

The mists swirled, obscuring their forms. "I will return," came the faint voice of Mr. Callan, "and when I do—"

Silence fell over them, interrupted only by the sound of their breathing.

Mary rushed to Mr. Huntley's side, gingerly touching the bruises on his face. "Mr. Huntley? Are you well?"

"I shall be fine, Miss Bennet," Mr. Huntley replied, taking her hand away from his face and holding it in both of his. "I am relieved to see you alive, Miss Bennet. You must have fared well against Miss Clarkson."

Mary nodded, unable to articulate what had occurred by the brook.

"The other two members of the Coven remain at large, I am afraid," said Mr. Huntley. "We must be prepared for another battle. Perhaps even more strenuous than this one."

Mary smiled. "I will be prepared. I require but a moment's rest to gather my strength."

From behind them came a shrill cackle. "'I require but a moment's rest to gather my strength.' Really my dear girl, you sound like a character from one of those novels you love so dearly."

Before either Mary or Mr. Huntley could act, Mr. Hartbustle swept toward them. A sudden bright light blinded Mary, but she could feel Mr. Huntley struggling unsuccessfully to keep hold of her hand. Then she sensed herself being lifted and swung onto someone's shoulder. A moment later Mary sank into darkness.

CHAPTER XVI

*W*hen Mary awoke she did not recognize her surroundings. Suppressing the urge to weep, she struggled to determine her location, but her clouded vision hindered her progress. Mary squeezed her eyes shut and then blinked several times. Upon opening them again, she experienced a moment's relief; her vision had cleared, and she knew exactly where Mr. Hartbustle had taken her: the small room at the back of his shop. She could not imagine how such a journey had been possible, yet here she was in London. She tried to raise herself off the floor, but her attempts to move were met with failure. Terror gripped her as she realized she was frozen in place.

"Mr. Hartbustle?" she called, her voice shaking despite her efforts to control it. When no one replied, she whispered, "Please?"

Someone nearby chuckled, but from Mary's position, she could not determine who it was until he spoke. "I apologize for our sudden departure. I see that I have caused you considerable discomfort. Rest assured, you will regain the use of your limbs. That spell has a different effect on everyone, so I cannot tell you *when* you shall feel improvements in your condition, but I give my word that you *will*."

Mary tried to gauge the direction of Mr. Hartbustle's voice. She thought it was coming from the back of the room. A tingling sensation in her fingers suggested that feeling was already returning to her body, but determining that surprise might prove to be her strongest ally, she did not wish to reveal that knowledge to Mr. Hartbustle.

"Miss Bennet, I must admit that I am terribly disappointed in you," Mr. Hartbustle said.

"For what reason, Mr. Hartbustle?" Mary was pleased to hear that she had regained control of her voice.

"I should think the answer is obvious," replied Mr. Hartbustle. Mary remained silent. "Perhaps not to you. I had such high hopes for you, dear Miss Bennet. You exhibited so much ambition and such hunger for magical knowledge. Add to those qualities your considerable talent, and I saw in you the potential to become a powerful member of the Bloomsbury Coven."

While Mr. Hartbustle spoke, Mary succeeded in rolling onto her stomach and pressing herself onto her forearms, allowing her a greater view of the room. Turning her head, she could see her captor sitting at the large meeting table, his chair angled away from her. In the shadowy light of the confined room, he looked small and frail, inspiring a wave of pity in Mary. She steeled herself against the emotion. Pity would only make her more vulnerable.

"You reminded me of myself," Mr. Hartbustle

mused. "So earnest and eager to learn." Hoping that Mr. Hartbustle was too occupied by his thoughts to notice, Mary began crawling in his direction. "My first impression of you was a favorable one; you were so deservedly pleased with yourself that you had managed to stop that thief. Then I was touched by your disappointment when you failed to find any magic books at my stall and so delighted by your reaction to the three books I showed you. I believe it was the joy lighting your face that first sparked my hope for your future with the Coven."

Mary continued her laborious journey across the floor toward Mr. Hartbustle, not certain what actions she would take when she reached him, but clinging to the notion that movement in any direction was better than remaining still. She had drawn within inches of the old man's chair when something heavy landed on her back. "Oh!" Mary cried as something sharp raked her skin.

At her outcry, Mr. Hartbustle turned to face her, and Mary recoiled in horror. Despite his wide smile, Mr. Hartbustle's usually twinkling eyes radiated a coldness that burned her.

"There, there, Mr. Spottiswoode! We must not hurt Miss Bennet. She must be kept safe and healthy until we have the book. We do not wish to tempt Mr. Huntley into any foolish actions, do we?"

Mary looked around the room, but saw only Mr. Hartbustle's cat sitting next to her cleaning his paws, pointedly ignoring the two humans. Had Mr. Hartbustle taken leave of his senses?

"Our friend appears confused, Spottiswoode. Perhaps you should show yourself."

Mary could not be certain, but she thought the cat

shrugged before standing and stretching luxuriously. A moment later Mary gasped. In the cat's place stood Mr. Spottiswoode. Blushing furiously, Mary turned away, for Mr. Spottiswoode seemed to have misplaced his clothing. Behind her Mr. Hartbustle erupted into a delighted laugh.

"Please clothe yourself, Spottiswoode. Our guest is overcome by her modesty."

Without speaking, Mr. Spottiswoode crossed behind the table. Mary watched his feet move across the floor.

"Come now, Miss Bennet. Exactly how did you imagine human-animal transformation spells work? You could hardly expect clothing to become fur," said Mr. Spottiswoode. "You should count yourself fortunate to witness such powerful magic," he added, pride filling his sharp voice.

Mary remained silent, too mortified by what she had just seen to formulate any thoughts. The desire to flee overtook her, and she cast a frightened glance around the room.

"I am afraid, Miss Bennet, that you will not reach the door unimpeded. Resign yourself to remaining our guest until Mr. Huntley arrives with the book."

Despite her fear, Mary bristled. "You shall never see that book again, Mr. Hartbustle," she said, indignation lending her courage.

"At last the girl speaks!" crowed Mr. Spottiswoode. "I thought maybe a—"

Mr. Hartbustle silenced him with a glance. "Why would you make such an assumption?" he asked Mary.

"Because we know why you desire it, and Mr. Huntley will do everything in his power to stop you!"

Her voice held more conviction than she felt.

Mr. Hartbustle's face fell, and for a moment Mary believed she had triumphed. But then he shook his head sadly and said, "Silly girl. I thought you were much wiser than that."

"What do you mean?" Mary asked.

"I mean Mr. Huntley is not so noble as you think. Perhaps I am gambling, Miss Bennet, but I believe that Mr. Huntley will arrive with the book in order to save *you* regardless of the threat he perceives from the Coven."

"But, but, I—" Mary began.

"Do you require additional explanation? I caught a glimpse of his face as I was sweeping you off to London. His expression told me everything. Mr. Huntley is in love with you, Miss Bennet, and the blush staining your cheeks reveals that his feelings are reciprocated. How charming! You are so naïve in matters of the heart, my dear, even with all that reading. I suppose your novels have taught you nothing."

Mr. Hartbustle paused and fixed his eyes on Mary, rendering her speechless. "I was once very like you, Miss Bennet," he mused. "Eager to demonstrate my worth and convinced of my moral and intellectual superiority. But when the time came for my trial, I was confronted with a very different set of truths. Oh, of course I was a skilled sorcerer, having demonstrated my proficiency at an early age. Great things were expected of me—after all, my grandfather founded the Bloomsbury Coven in the fifteenth century."

Mary was stunned by this revelation. Perhaps Christopher Marlowe *had* meant this Mr. Hartbustle!

Mr. Hartbustle chuckled. "Despite my talent, like you, I had no idea what true power was within my reach—until my trial."

Curiosity overwhelmed her, and Mary could not help but ask, "What was your trial?"

"Ah, Miss Bennet, you are forcing me to revise my opinion of you once again. I am impressed that even in the face of mortal danger, your inquisitiveness refuses to be suppressed!"

"But you just told Mr. Spottiswoode that I am to be kept safe," Mary replied.

Mr. Hartbustle laughed. "Indeed, I did," he said, and for a moment Mary saw a glimmer of her friend as she had known him. "How clever of you! At any rate, it would hardly be hospitable of me to deny you an answer. And I believe a story would help us pass the time while we await Mr. Huntley's arrival."

"Hartbustle! How can you share this story with *her*? An untested, unqualified *outsider*?" Mr. Spottiswoode protested.

"I have my reasons, Edmund," Mr. Hartbustle replied. "I shall thank you for allowing me to continue."

Mr. Spottiswoode subsided, his agitation clear nevertheless. Mary chose to ignore the icy stare he fixed upon her, placing her full attention on Mr. Hartbustle.

"I was merely eighteen years of age, perhaps too young, some said. My father, however, could not have been more proud of me. I met my trial with all the confidence you might expect from a young man too ignorant to acknowledge the risks. I had been given the fascinating task of recreating the recipe for the Ancient Welsh Ale of Delirium and then using it to move beyond the boundaries of conscious thought. It took considerable time and much effort. And not a little mess. But at last I perfected my brew and could walk in the spirit realms."

"What did you see there?" Mary, her situation almost forgotten, was all eagerness.

"How dare you ask that question? Mr. Hartbustle, I must protest. You have already revealed too much!" Mr. Spottiswoode exclaimed, a vein throbbing in his temple.

"Poor, dear Edmund," said Mr. Hartbustle shaking his head. "You have always guarded our secrets so jealously. But you must trust that I have a reason for sharing this tale. It is after all *mine* to tell. Please keep your peace; I will not ask again." Mr. Hartbustle's voice had sharpened, causing Mr. Spottiswoode to drop his head and stare at the floor.

"I found the journey through the spirit realms fascinating. A whole host of sensations assailed me—even now I cannot make sense of the more vivid of the visions, although fragments of memories made of swirling colors and beautiful music haunt me still.

"Then, just before the effects of my brew wore off, I came across something that startled me out of myself. I saw an immense force; it seemed to breathe, so alive it was. At first I had no idea what lay before me. It was shapeless—a dark mass—but it exuded such raw energy, and it drew me to it. Gradually I began to understand what it was. There is great power at our fingertips, Miss Bennet, power that my grandfather and father were too squeamish to touch. A great, terrible, dark power beyond the little spells we use to move items through the air or to conjure hot water for tea."

A memory stirred in Mary's mind. Again she stood on the precipice of her dream, desire to touch that dark power welling up in her.

"What is it, Miss Bennet? All the color has drained from your face," said Mr. Hartbustle.

"I—I saw it, too," she said, her voice barely a whisper.

A savage smile spread across Mr. Hartbustle's face. "So you understand. You are more like me than I could have hoped."

"No!" Mary cried.

"Do not deny it, Miss Bennet. If you have shared that vision, you understand. Until my trial I had no idea how I hungered for *more*. More control. More power. And what I saw offered that to me, as it will to you. I knew then what I had to do. I had to find the books that could teach me the words I needed to gain access to that power, and then I would be *free*."

"Indeed?" came another voice. "Books such as this one?" Mr. Huntley stood framed in the doorway.

CHAPTER XVII

"Mr. Huntley!" cried Mary. "You must leave at once! Take the book and go!" She started to run toward him, but Mr. Spottiswoode caught her, pinning her arms behind her back. She struggled against her captivity, but to no avail. Mr. Spottiswoode's strength more than surpassed hers.

As Mary cried her warning, Mr. Hartbustle rushed toward the door. Mr. Huntley, distracted by Mary's cries, only narrowly escaped, racing backward into the bookshop. He succeeded, however, in drawing Mr. Hartbustle out of the small room and away from Mary. "Miss Bennet!" he called. "Have they caused you any harm?"

Mr. Hartbustle, still advancing toward Mr. Huntley, laughed. "So gallant, Huntley! But you need not worry; Miss Bennet remained perfectly safe with us."

"I shall be more convinced if that brute releases her into my care," Mr. Huntley replied, his composure restored.

"And if Spottiswoode fails to comply with your desires?"

"If you do not free Miss Bennet, I shall destroy the book, Hartbustle."

Mary held her breath, waiting for Mr. Hartbustle's reply. She could not understand why Mr. Huntley had not *already* destroyed the book, but she supposed he must have had a good reason.

Mr. Hartbustle, who had been steadily closing the gap between himself and Mr. Huntley, stopped. Mary could hear the smile in his voice as he responded to Mr. Huntley. "Really, Huntley. Please do not insult me with such an obvious lie. You have had ample opportunities to destroy the book; why should I believe your threat? No, Alfred, if you meant to destroy it, you would have done so by now. I suspect you cling to it for much the same reason I desire its return."

Craning her neck, Mary could see Mr. Huntley. An odd expression crossed his face.

"I see I have hit upon something!" crowed Mr. Hartbustle. Mary thought he enjoyed taunting Mr. Huntley. "I see the Palimpsest Spell. You chose to hide the book rather than to eliminate it. Why is that?"

Mr. Huntley, recovering control over his countenance, refused to answer. Mary felt the tension between the two men increase. Something dark and savage was taking shape between Mr. Huntley and Mr. Hartbustle. It terrified her, but she longed to be free to help Mr. Huntley. Instead she could only watch.

"Shall I answer for you? You could no more destroy that book than you could take a human life.

At least that is the noble response, is it not, Mr. Huntley? But there lurks a far nastier truth inside that honorable exterior. You cannot bear to part with the book because of the secrets it contains—secrets that bring with them immeasurable power. You covet power, Huntley. No sorcerer is immune."

Mary could not understand why Mr. Huntley did nothing. How could he simply stand and listen to Mr. Hartbustle's accusations? "That is not true, Mr. Hartbustle!" Mary cried, resuming her struggle against Mr. Spottiswoode. "Tell him, Mr. Huntley!"

"Will you lie to the girl, too, Huntley?" sneered Hartbustle.

"I am afraid, Miss Bennet, that he speaks the truth. You know it to be so."

Mary gasped, amazement arresting her efforts against Mr. Spottiswoode's grip. "No," she breathed.

"So you admit it?"

"I cannot lie to her. But Miss Bennet," continued Mr. Huntley, "what a sorcerer does with that desire is up to him. Unlike Mr. Hartbustle who has succumbed to it, I fight against it. You see what has happened to him. We all have a choice."

"All this time with the book, Huntley, and you mean to tell me that you have never been tempted by the power of Blood Magic?" Mr. Hartbustle's disbelief was etched into his voice. "Or are you afraid?"

"No, Hartbustle. I am no coward; I simply draw my power from other sources," said Mr. Huntley, conjuring a ball of bright light, which he threw at Mr. Hartbustle.

Mr. Hartbustle reacted immediately, deflecting the orb and sending it across the store where it landed harmlessly on the floor and disappeared. "The golden orb! My word, Huntley, you have demonstrated enormous growth. And it almost touched me—that would have been painful indeed!"

"Not painful, Hartbustle, fatal. I modified the spell so that upon contact the orb would penetrate your skin and burn you from the inside out. Should you still be in possession of a soul, even that would be devoured."

"An impressive feat! But such meanness is beneath you, Alfred. Of course I am still in possession of a soul. Mr. Marlowe took liberties with my story, and for that he paid dearly."

In the other room Mary had grown impatient with the battle's lack of progress. Her frustration lent her strength. Taking a deep breath, she stomped on Mr. Spottiswoode's left foot and then thrust her elbow into his plump midsection. With a grunt, Spottiswoode released her and doubled over in obvious discomfort. Free from his clutches, Mary raced forward into the shop. Stopping just behind Mr. Hartbustle, she shouted, "Bind—"

Mr. Hartbustle, all pretense of affability gone, rushed towards her, growling, "Enough!" With a flick of his hand, he banished the tendrils of mist that had begun curling around him. "You will not use that spell against me, Miss Bennet. Your arrogance has lost its charm." Mr. Hartbustle pointed at her, and Mary felt as though someone pushed her with great force back toward the small room.

"Hartbustle! Leave Miss Bennet and I shall give you the book," called Mr. Huntley.

"I have already shown a great deal of patience," Mr. Hartbustle replied, turning back toward Mr. Huntley. "Do not try it further by making such demands of me. I will have that book, and then I will punish you both for daring to defy me!"

Mary's heart stopped when she heard a loud crash from the shop. Fearing for the worst, she called, "Mr. Huntley!"

"Stay where you are, Miss Bennet! I am not—" Another crash interrupted him.

Free from the invisible hand's pressure, Mary started to move back toward the battle, anxious to assure herself of Mr. Huntley's safety. Mr. Spottiswoode, who had recovered from her assault, grasped one of her hands, arresting her progress. This time she managed to slip away from his poor grip, and turning, threw a ball of fire toward him. But the fire missed Mr. Spottiswoode and caught hold of some papers lying on the table. Soon smoke filled the small room, and Mary had to drop to her knees and crawl toward the door. When she reached it, Mary looked back and saw that Spottiswoode had transformed into a cat. Though she started to close the door to trap him in the burning room, he managed to escape, streaking through the shop out into Lamb's Conduit Street where he disappeared. Moments later Mary heard cracking wood; the fire had already gained considerable strength.

"Spottiswoode, like any cat, was loyal only to himself. Sometimes I wondered if he stayed with me simply for the bowls of cream I supplied. I see now that I was correct. Never mind," Hartbustle said. With ease, he doused the fire before directing a bust of David Garrick to fly toward Mr. Huntley, who dodged it just in time and watched it shatter when it hit the floor behind him. Mr. Huntley sat panting for a moment before rising. To retaliate, he commanded a ladder to soar toward Mr. Hartbustle and trap him against one of the bookcases lining the shop's walls.

Crying, "Blast!" Mr. Hartbustle freed himself, propelling splinters around the shop.

Mary dropped to the ground, barely avoiding a large piece of the ladder that passed over her head and collided with the wall behind her. Scrambling to her feet, Mary faced Hartbustle, concentrated on her intention, and shouted, "Obscure—" But something gripped her throat, cutting off her speech; she opened her mouth to gasp for air, but none would come.

"A brave attempt, Miss Bennet," said Mr. Hartbustle. "However, you are not quick enough." He stood several feet away, left hand clenched in a fist.

Panic rose, threatening to overtake Mary. She clawed at her throat in fruitless attempts to loosen the vise from around her neck. With each moment she grew fainter.

"Not so clever after all, are you Miss Bennet?" said Mr. Hartbustle, advancing toward her.

Behind him, Mr. Huntley placed a finger to his lips. At the golden orb in Mr. Huntley's palm, Mary's eyes widened despite her attempts to control her demeanor. Unfortunately, Mr. Hartbustle noticed her eyes and turned. Instead of hitting him in the back, the orb glanced off Mr. Hartbustle's leg with just enough force to knock him off balance. He threw his hands out to catch himself, releasing Mary from his spell.

As Mary lay on the floor drawing great breaths, the world came back into focus. She could see Mr. Hartbustle examining the wound caused by Mr. Huntley's golden orb, but she could not find Mr. Huntley.

"You must be so disappointed, Huntley. Your clever modification failed. The orb left only the smallest flesh wound. I believe I shall survive."

Then Mary could no longer understand the words pouring from Mr. Hartbustle's mouth. She followed his intense glare and saw Mr. Huntley on the floor, writhing. Something red dotted his clothing. As the red patches grew, Mary realized that he was bleeding, but why she could not comprehend. Forgetting everything except Mr. Huntley's wounds, Mary rushed to his side. There she worked feverishly to stop the bleeding, pulling off her pelisse and holding it to as many red patches as she could.

"Come!" called Mr. Hartbustle. Mary looked up, but too late. She tried to catch the book as it careened across the shop and into Mr. Hartbustle's hands. "Best tend to his wounds, Miss Bennet. I believe he is in some mortal danger."

Mary looked down and was dismayed by what she saw. Mr. Huntley had lost consciousness. She leaned over to determine if he was still breathing. After a momentary panic, she was relieved to feel a delicate breath against her cheek. Concentrating all her energy on Mr. Huntley, she tried to will him to live. She could see that she was on the brink of failure.

But then her attention was again diverted by Mr. Hartbustle. He stood reading from *Blood Magicks*, muttering words Mary could not hear. As he spoke, Mr. Hartbustle began to change. He grew to almost twice his height, his body outlined with a malignant yellow glow. The light grew stronger, and Mary felt herself weaken. Terror blossomed in her stomach as she realized that Mr. Hartbustle had begun to draw the world's magic from other sorcerers. If Mary did not act quickly, both she and Mr. Huntley would die.

Mastering the fear that threatened to overcome her, Mary cast her eyes around the shop, searching for a weapon. Catching sight of a thick book on a shelf directly above Mr. Hartbustle, Mary concentrated all of her energy and sent the book flying with as much force as she could toward the rapidly altering Mr. Hartbustle. It hit him hard in the center of his back, knocking him forward. He lost his balance and fell, his chin striking the desk in front of him, which caused his head to snap back with a sickening crunch. Mary watched, appalled, as Mr. Hartbustle slid to the ground. For several moments she stood, unable to believe what had happened. Eventually Mary recovered herself and knelt next to Mr. Hartbustle on the floor. His head angled impossibly from his body, and his eyes, which had been darting frantically around the shop, had gone suddenly still and empty. Mr. Hartbustle was dead. With a pang of sorrow for the friend he had once been, Mary reached over and closed his eyes. Bowing her head, she caught sight of the book that had proved to be such a fatal weapon: James Fordyce's *Sermons to Young Women*.

"Miss Bennet?" whispered Mr. Huntley.

Forgetting Mr. Hartbustle, Mary rushed to Mr. Huntley's side. "I am here, Mr. Huntley. You need not worry."

"Hartbustle?"

"Dead," Mary said. "He cannot hurt you any further."

Mr. Huntley laughed, wincing at the pain it caused him. Alarmed by the blood still seeping from Mr. Huntley's wounds, Mary reached out and took Mr. Huntley's hand, holding it tightly as she leaned over him and stroked his hair back from his forehead, now beaded with perspiration. "What has he done to you?" she asked.

"He used a Welsh healing spell for blood letting, but he altered two syllables in the incantation, which turned it deadly," Mr. Huntley murmured. "It seems Mr. Hartbustle spoke fluent Welsh."

Desperation flooded through Mary as she asked, "What do I do to stop it? How do I help you?"

Mr. Huntley did not answer.

"Mr. Huntley! Mr. Huntley!" Mary cried, but to no avail. Mr. Huntley had again lost consciousness. A strange sensation passed through Mary: her panic had been transformed to anger. She had not suffered through two battles and caused the deaths of two people to allow Mr. Huntley to die. No. She was a powerful sorceress, and she would find a way to save him. Closing her eyes, Mary took a breath to compose herself. Another steadying breath slowed Mary's frantic heart, and in the stillness, she realized what she must do.

She opened her eyes and rushed to Mr. Hartbustle's side to retrieve *Blood Magicks*. Dropping back to her knees, she thumbed hastily through the book until she came to the section entitled "Blood Healing." Glancing back at Mr. Huntley, she gasped. Blood had begun pooling around his body and a thin red river had started trickling toward her. Hurriedly, she skimmed the list of healing spells until she found one that she felt would work: the Blood for Blood spell, which required the sacrifice of her blood to save Mr. Huntley's life. Mary counted that an equal exchange. Before returning to Mr. Huntley's side to perform the spell, she raced around Mr. Hartbustle's shop gathering the items she would need for the ritual bloodletting. On the desk she was fortunate enough to find a piece of chalk and a small knife. Then she snatched a teacup from the table at the back of the shop and hurried back to Mr. Huntley's side.

With the chalk she traced a hasty circle around them both and then knelt next to Mr. Huntley. Without flinching, she drew the knife across the soft, white flesh of her forearm, making a shallow cut that would nonetheless yield enough blood to work the spell. Placing the teacup under her arm to catch the blood, she began chanting the words of the spell, "Blood for blood," over and over again under her breath. When she began to feel faint, she bound her arm with a piece of cloth torn from her petticoat. Then it was time to perform the spell's final element—somehow Mary would have to set her blood on fire.

Ignoring the distressing thought that she had no idea what to do next, Mary focused all her energy on the blood gathered in the small teacup and imagined it bursting into flame. Nothing happened. Next she summoned a fireball and dropped it into the cup, but the blood doused the flame upon contact, leaving only a tiny puff of smoke. Nearly weeping as her frustration mounted, Mary stared at the blood and shouted, "Burn! Burn!" She was on the brink of collapse when she noticed that the blood had begun to boil. Heartened by this development, she tried again. "Burn!" she cried, and scarlet flames leapt from the teacup.

As Mary watched the fire in amazement, she felt a hand upon her arm. She looked down to see Mr. Huntley smiling up at her. With total disregard for the rules of polite society, Mary leaned over and kissed Mr. Huntley squarely on the mouth. They were denied all opportunities for embarrassment, however, as immediately thereafter the fire, fuelled by the magical energies lingering in the shop, began to spread. The tiny porcelain cup, unable to withstand the fire's force, shattered. Mary threw herself over Mr. Huntley to protect him from the flying shards.

"We must leave, Mr. Huntley," exclaimed Mary as a spark from the fire alighted on a book and caused an entire bookcase to ignite with a great whoosh. Cradling *Blood Magicks* in one arm, she reached down to help Mr. Huntley.

"What has happened?" he asked while he struggled to his feet.

The fire began to spread. "I shall explain later! We must go!" cried Mary, pushing Mr. Huntley toward the door. The fire followed behind them, beginning to devour everything in its path. They reached the door just as the fire spread into the front of the shop. With a great effort, Mary leapt forward and then turned to pull Mr. Huntley through the door.

"Wait!" he cried as Mary tried to pull him along the street. With obvious effort he gathered his strength. Fixing his eyes on the clouds above, he shouted "Deluge!" Before Mary had time to wonder at his behavior, she felt thick drops of rain. A moment later, they were soaked, and steam began rising as the rain hit the fire. Soon it would be completely extinguished. Resisting the urge to collapse, Mary helped Mr. Huntley down the street, across a busy thoroughfare, past the foundling hospital, and into a sheltered garden in Mecklenburgh Square. There they were finally able to rest. Panting, they dropped to the ground.

CHAPTER XVIII

*M*ary and Mr. Huntley lay in silence, cushioned by the garden's soft grass. The rain that had been falling in sheets on the bookshop was here just a light drizzle. In the distance they could hear a commotion, presumably caused by the fire and sudden downpour in Lamb's Conduit Street. Mary felt a pang of guilt for the destruction of Mr. Hartbustle's shop. But then Mr. Huntley stirred, and her mind was otherwise occupied. Looking over at Mr. Huntley, she was relieved to see his color returning. He sat up and she followed suit.

Suddenly the enormity of what had happened that day struck her, and she began to sob. Mr. Huntley grasped her hand and kissed it, saying, "My dear Miss Bennet, how brave you have been! Had it not been for you, I never would have survived Mr. Hartbustle's attack. You saved me, Miss Bennet. For that I shall be forever grateful. More importantly, you stopped Mr. Hartbustle and assured the safety of this book. The world owes you a tremendous debt."

Mary attempted a smile through her tears, but failed, for her mind refused to stop fixing on images that made her quiver: the Horned Hounds materializing in the woods, Mr. Hartbustle's empty eyes staring at nothing, and Mr. Huntley lying in a pool of his own blood. Nothing she had ever read could have prepared her for this day's harrowing events. But her misery was softened by gratitude as Mr. Huntley waited patiently for her to regain her composure, sitting calmly at her side holding her hand.

When Mary had at last collected herself, she dried her eyes, reluctantly releasing Mr. Huntley's hand to do so, and asked, "What do we do now, Mr. Huntley?"

"We return home, Miss Bennet," replied Mr. Huntley.

"But how? We have no coach, and I have no money. How will we get back to Hertfordshire? It is a day's journey at least. Oh! Whatever will I tell my family? They will think that I have disappeared! Perhaps they will believe that I have run away with you, and that I am no different from Lydia!" The idea that she could be compared to her youngest sister produced another round of tears. A full minute passed before Mary was calm enough to hear Mr. Huntley's reply.

"I assure you, Miss Bennet, we require neither coach nor money to return home," said Mr. Huntley. "I will need your help, as I have yet to recover my strength."

Intrigued, Mary forgot her tears. "Shall we fly?" she asked.

Mr. Huntley smiled. "No, nothing quite so

exhilarating, I am afraid. We shall use the Folding Spell."

"Indeed?" Mary could not believe what Mr. Huntley had suggested. She had read about this complicated spell that allowed sorcerers to cross great distances in a single step. The spell's description made it sound far simpler than it was: *If one desires to move from London to Kent, for example, one merely folds the space between the locations and steps lightly from one to the next.* She did not understand what "fold the space between" meant, but she could tell that this was magic beyond the abilities of most sorcerers.

"Are you familiar with the spell?"

"Oh, yes! But I never imagined anyone could *perform* it!"

"I believe Mr. Hartbustle conveyed you to London with it, and after I freed myself from his binding spell and retrieved *Blood Magicks*, I followed by the same means," Mr. Huntley explained.

Wretchedness transformed to excitement, and Mary beamed, her tear-stained face glowing with anticipation.

"I shall assume that you mean to help me," said Mr. Huntley, laughing.

Mary nodded.

"Excellent!" he exclaimed, standing. Helping Mary to her feet, he continued, "The incantation is simple: 'Fold London into Hertfordshire.' But the spell requires a great deal of energy and strength. I am lacking in both at the moment, especially after calling the rain, so I shall rely upon you, Miss Bennet, to provide them."

"And what would you have me do?"

"Hold my hand and imagine the lawn outside the

vicarage. See it in your mind in every detail. Then, when I squeeze your hand, say the words with me."

Mary nodded and reached for Mr. Huntley's hand. When she took it she felt a shock at the power they exchanged. Buoyed by this power, she turned her mind toward the lawn outside the vicarage and pictured every detail from the hydrangea bushes flanking the front door to the hedgerow lining the grass. When she felt Mr. Huntley squeeze her hand, she said in a clear voice, "Fold London into Hertfordshire."

Because she felt nothing happen, Mary worried that the spell had not worked, but when she opened her eyes, she saw the vicarage in front of her and turning her head, saw Mecklenburgh Square behind her. Amazed, she took a step forward with Mr. Huntley, and the quiet garden in Bloomsbury disappeared. They had arrived home.

***

"You have returned!" came the relieved voice of Mrs. Huntley when Mary and Mr. Huntley stepped inside the vicarage. The vicar's mother appeared in the vestibule and immediately ushered them into the parlor. Mary felt as though her legs could not carry her much farther and was relieved to sink into one of the comfortable chairs by the fire.

"I shall send for tea," said Mrs. Huntley as soon as she had wrapped a blanket around Mary's shivering form. "Alfred, sit down and rest! You look dreadful."

As his mother hurried from the room, Mr. Huntley obeyed her command, dropping into the chair opposite Mary. "How do you feel?" he asked.

"As though the room is turning rather rapidly, but at least I have managed to remain conscious," Mary replied.

"Probably because you knew the shift was coming. Only when it is unexpected does the spell result in a loss of consciousness."

"Alfred, you must allow Miss Bennet to rest!" Mrs. Huntley returned to the parlor followed by the housekeeper bearing a tea tray. The three waited in silence as Mrs. Owens served the tea.

"Alfred, you look dreadful," Mrs. Huntley repeated as soon as Mrs. Owens had left them alone.

"I imagine I do," he replied.

"I suppose there is a lengthy explanation," she said.

The sun had begun to set by the time Mr. Huntley and Mary finished relating all that had transpired in London. Mrs. Huntley betrayed very little of her anxiety during the narration, but Mary noticed the force with which the vicar's mother gripped her chair as her son explained the bruises on his face and the blood staining his clothing.

"Had it not been for Miss Bennet and her cool head, I certainly could not have survived," he admitted.

"I am grateful, Miss Bennet, for your presence in London, although I wish for your sake that it had not been necessary," said Mrs. Huntley. "And now we must dress that wound on your arm properly and then see you home with a suitable excuse for your long absence from Longbourn."

Less than a quarter of an hour later, Mrs. Huntley presented a note to Mary for her approval.

Dear Mrs. Bennet,

I beg your forgiveness for detaining your daughter at the vicarage for the entire afternoon. My son was taken away on business, leaving me quite alone with a slight cold. He encountered Miss Bennet in the lane and entreated her to pay me a visit, knowing as he does how I enjoy her company. I am afraid I caused the visit to extend quite beyond the boundaries of what is considered polite. She was terribly kind to indulge an old woman who loves to tell stories about her life, and for that kindness I shall remain forever grateful.

Yours in friendship,

Mrs. E. Huntley

"Will that suffice?" Mrs. Huntley asked as Mary looked up.

A smile spread across Mary's face. "I think it will."

"Excellent. Now, Alfred, you must change your clothes and do something to hide those dreadful bruises before you accompany Miss Bennet to Longbourn. Do limit yourself to a short visit. You require dinner and rest."

***

Mrs. Bennet was all astonishment when Mary entered the parlor with the vicar.

"Mary, where have you been?" she asked, struggling to contain her agitation.

"I have passed the day at the vicarage, Mama," said Mary. "Anticipating your concern, Mrs. Huntley sent this note to excuse my absence from home."

Mrs. Bennet accepted the note, and after studying her daughter for a moment, read it. "My word!" she cried when she finished. "Spent the entire day with Mrs. Huntley? By *Mr.* Huntley's request?" At the coyness in her mother's voice, Mary blushed.

"Indeed, Mrs. Bennet. I regret that my duties took me away, robbing me of the pleasure of Miss Bennet's company."

"Oh my!" cried Mrs. Bennet. "Sit down, Mr. Huntley. Please."

"Again I must express my regret. My mother awaits me at the vicarage. But I would like to call on you tomorrow, Miss Bennet, if that is convenient for you?"

"I look forward to it, Mr. Huntley," Mary replied.

"Excellent. Well then, I shall see you tomorrow. Good night, Miss Bennet. Mrs. Bennet. Mr. Bennet." Mr. Huntley bowed to each Bennet in turn before taking his leave.

"My word, Mary!" cried Mrs. Bennet as soon as Mr. Huntley disappeared into the hall. "I do believe the vicar has fallen in love with you! I never would have believed it if I had not seen it with my own eyes. But how he looked at you! Oh, my Lord! They say he has at least ten thousand a year, Mary. Just think of it! Ten thousand a year in addition to his living in the parish. And his mother's uncle was a *baronet*!"

Mary turned to her father, who nodded and intervened on her behalf. "My dear, do you not think you have leapt to conclusions? The banns have yet to be read."

"Mr. Bennet, did you not see how he gazed on her?" came the heated reply.

"No, I did not, for his back was to me for most of his visit. But can you not see that your daughter is made uncomfortable by your effusions?" Mr. Bennet looked closely at his daughter. "Mary, because your mother is occupied by her rapturous imagination, I excuse you for the evening. You must go to your room and sleep, my dear. You appear spent."

"Thank you, Papa," said Mary, relieved. Bidding her mother an unheard good night, Mary went to her room where she collapsed into her bed and sank into a deep and dreamless sleep.

CHAPTER XIX

A night of uninterrupted sleep restored Mary almost entirely to her usual self. In the morning she joined her family, eager for breakfast. Her parents had just taken their places at the table when Mary arrived.

"You look much better, Mary," said Mr. Bennet as Mary took her seat.

"I feel a good deal better, Papa."

"I trust you slept well?"

"I did, thank you, Papa," replied Mary as she added milk to her tea.

"Very good," said Mr. Bennet.

Mrs. Bennet watched their exchange with a look of growing impatience. Finally unable to hold her tongue, she spoke. "Is that all you can talk about? Mary, the vicar is calling for you today. Is that of no importance?"

"Of course it is important, my dear," said Mr. Bennet, "but the poor girl should be allowed to break her fast in peace before you begin your inquisition."

Mary did not attempt to hide her smile. She

enjoyed watching her father tease her mother, especially as he did so on her behalf, just as he had done for Lizzy. Mrs. Bennet refused to be distracted from her pursuit.

"Mr. Bennet, how can you tease me when I have only her future well-being in mind? You do not share my concerns for her happiness."

"On the contrary, Mrs. Bennet, my concern surpasses yours. At least I do not embarrass the poor girl in front of the vicar. Let her be, my dear Mrs. Bennet."

"But I—" Mrs. Bennet began, puffed with indignation.

"Mama, please," said Mary. "All will be well." The strength of Mary's tone completely arrested Mrs. Bennet's speech. The breakfast parlor remained quiet for several moments.

"Well, I suppose you know what is best," said Mrs. Bennet at last. Then she rose and hurried from the room.

"Perhaps I should not have spoken to her with such sharpness," said Mary.

"Do not worry, Mary. Your mother will no doubt recover as soon as your engagement is announced."

Mary looked at her father in disbelief.

"Dear child, I received a note from Mr. Huntley this morning. I was not to mention it to you, but I do understand what it portends. And here is the young man himself," said Mr. Bennet as Mr. Huntley entered the breakfast parlor.

Mary knew a blush had spread across her cheeks, but she did not mind. She had grown used to the sensation.

"Good morning, Mr. Huntley," said Mr. Bennet.

"The day looks fine; perhaps you and Mary would like a walk in the garden? Our little wilderness has grown quite interesting in the past several months."

"Of course, Papa, an excellent idea," said Mary, rising to leave. "Mr. Huntley, shall we go?"

With a nod, Mr. Huntley offered his arm, which Mary took. Mr. Bennet winked at her, smiling broadly. As she left the room, Mary heard him chuckling.

Having experienced enough of the Longbourn wilderness, Mary and Mr. Huntley chose instead to follow the more orderly garden paths. A large shrubbery ensured their privacy.

"You look well this morning, Miss Bennet," said Mr. Huntley as they turned into the garden.

"Thank you, Mr. Huntley," Mary replied. "As do you. How are your injuries?"

"My wounds have already begun to heal. As you saw, my mother has some knowledge of the physician's art."

Mary nodded, absently touching her arm. "Is she a sorceress? I never thought to ask you."

"She is not, but her uncle, the baronet, was a sorcerer, and he taught her some simple potions and remedies. My mother has many interests and talents, and though she has no magical abilities, she is an accomplished healer. When we lived in India, she often assisted the village wise men in their work. I suppose some of their magic may have transferred to her, although how I do not know, but her prowess as a healer has increased over the years."

"And your father? Was he a sorcerer?"

"Indeed. A very fine one. I believe he would have been very helpful to us had he lived, but he perished several years ago in India." Mr. Huntley's silence told Mary that he did not wish to speak further about his father. She contented herself with strolling alongside him.

At the end of the garden lane, they came to a stone bench. Mary, feeling a slight fatigue come over her, stopped and sat down. Mr. Huntley sat next to her.

"Miss Bennet, yesterday's distressing events must weigh heavily on your mind," Mr. Huntley said, his voice gentle. "If—if I may be of any aid to you in—in—"

"Thank you, Mr. Huntley. I find your presence very comforting," Mary said, blushing. "In time I shall recover from what I saw..." She paused, weighing her words. "But I have a confession to make. Mr. Huntley, do you remember that dream I described to you?

Mr. Huntley nodded.

"I was not entirely honest with you in my account of its details. You see, when I looked into that wicked power, I felt—hungry. My ambition was roused, and it filled me with a great need to touch that darkness. I could not tell you this before because I did not entirely understand it. But now I know. I had a choice, and although in my dream I chose the dark, when I awoke I chose the light." She paused again, a troubled expression on her face.

"Yet you worry about what you might do when faced with that choice again, do you not, Miss Bennet?"

Mary nodded, a tear sliding down her cheek. "The power—it tempted me so." With an impatient gesture, she wiped the tear away. "Mr. Huntley, I have lived my entire life in the shadows of my sisters. They are all more beautiful, more engaging, more charming. I had only my books and music to set myself apart; even then I was overshadowed. Elizabeth was always the far superior musician, and she possessed a keener wit. But then your book arrived, and I discovered something that would allow me to shine the brightest. For once..." Mary trailed off, ashamed by what she had revealed.

Mr. Huntley slid from the bench and knelt in front of her. Taking both her hands in his, he said, "Miss Bennet, when I watched you battle the Coven, I was amazed by your strength and courage. Knowing that you resisted a dreadful temptation, to which even the most powerful sorcerers succumb, merely raises you in my already considerable estimation. Your bravery, talent, and remarkable capacity to remain calm in the face of daunting circumstances raise you above not only most women, but also most men. In short, Miss Bennet, I believe you to be a truly remarkable woman."

Before she could reply, he leaned in and kissed her. It was the sweetest moment of Mary's young life.

"Miss Bennet," said Mr. Huntley softly. "I have loved you for quite some time, and I hope I do not flatter myself in believing that you share my sentiments."

Mary, unable to speak, gave an enthusiastic nod.

In response, Mr. Huntley smiled and said, "Would you, Miss Bennet, do me the great honor of consenting to be my wife?"

Mary's heart leapt. "Yes, Mr. Huntley," she replied. A second kiss seemed called for.

"Now, Miss Bennet, I should like to speak with your father. Shall we return to the house?"

Elated, Mary rose and took his arm.

"Has Mr. Huntley returned to the vicarage already?" asked a disappointed Mrs. Bennet as Mary entered the drawing room alone.

"No, Mama. He is in the library speaking with Papa," Mary replied, sitting in her favorite chair near the fire.

"Indeed?" cried Mrs. Bennet.

Mary nodded and opened her book. She tried to give it her full attention, but her thoughts remained with Mr. Huntley and her father.

"Oh my word! Do you suppose…could it be? But that is impossible. You have done nothing to encourage him. Why would he—?" The two gentlemen entered the drawing room, interrupting Mrs. Bennet's speculation with their power either to confirm or to deny her fondest wish.

"Well, Mary, it seems congratulations are in order," said Mr. Bennet taking a seat opposite Mrs. Bennet as Mr. Huntley sat in the chair opposite Mary.

"Thank you, Papa," replied Mary.

"What do you mean, Mr. Bennet?" asked Mrs. Bennet.

"I have just given Mr. Huntley permission to wed Mary, my dear. It seems soon enough we shall find Longbourn terribly empty." Mary smiled as her father did not sound so disheartened by the idea.

"Mr. Huntley!" cried Mrs. Bennet, somewhat overcome by her emotions. "Lord bless me! I never thought I would see the day. A wedding for Mary! I shall have to tell Lady Lucas! Will she not be terribly disappointed! Oh, please excuse me, Mr. Huntley. I have so much to do!" And still chattering to herself about wedding clothes, Mrs. Bennet hurried out of the room.

A moment later Mr. Huntley stood. "I am afraid I shall have to take my leave as well," he said. "My mother will wish to hear the news." He smiled at Mary.

"Of course," she said, returning his smile.

"I shall call for you again tomorrow morning," he said before leaving.

Mary and her father sat in silence for a few minutes. "You have done well, Mary," said Mr. Bennet at length.

"I know, Papa."

"He is much less silly than many gentlemen his age. Especially for a sorcerer."

"I beg your pardon, Papa. Did you just say—?"

"Indeed. Perhaps one day you will relate the events of the past few days to me. But for now I should like nothing more than to enjoy the quiet."

"Of course Papa," said Mary. And with a full heart, she returned to her book.

FIN

ACKNOWLEDGMENTS

This novella began its life as a silly little story I wrote one day in a café. Many people both living and not had a hand in giving it a more substantial life. Without Jane Austen's marvelous *Pride and Prejudice*, I would have no Mary Bennet, no Mr. Bennet and no Longbourn. Without J. K. Rowling's fantastically imagined world of Harry Potter, I would have had no rich source for the Regency Magic series. So my first thanks go to these authors. For the idea that Mary could develop a taste for the lowly novel, I thank Craig Gleason Neibaur. A few years ago we were in a production of *Pride and Prejudice*—him as Wickham, me as Mary—and a back stage joke about Wickham's desire to ingratiate himself with the whole family made it into the first pages of this book. My wonderful readers Christine Kam-Lynch, Kim Street, Linda Deitchman, and my husband Dave Peticolas gave generously of their time and energy, pointing out inconsistencies, repetitions, and errors. Dave deserves thanks for a great many other things including his unfailing support of all that I do. Finally, to my writing partner and fellow Luminous Creature, Emily June Street, I owe a tremendous debt of gratitude for her insightful (and patient) reading of draft after draft. Without her, Mary would never have had this adventure. Neither would I.

ABOUT THE AUTHOR

Beth Deitchman wrote her first book, *Behind Every Great Man There's a Great Cat*, when she was in third grade. After that she took some time off from writing to pursue other interests. While her plans to be a ballerina and manager of the Pittsburgh Pirates fell through, she did have short careers in both ballet and modern dance. She's also been a lecturer in English at UC Davis and an actor. These days Beth teaches Pilates in Northern California where she lives with her husband, Dave, and dog, Ralphie. And she's back to writing, having realized that nothing else is quite so satisfying.

Follow @beth_deitchman on Twitter
www.bethdeitchman.com
www.luminouscreaturespress.com

Read more Regency Magic in Margeret Dashwood and the Enchanted Atlas from LCP!

Mary Bennet and the Bloomsbury Coven

Beth Deitchman

Mary Bennet and the Bloomsbury Coven

Made in the USA
San Bernardino, CA
08 November 2014